GHOST AND BONE

GHOST AND BONE

ANDREW PRENTICE

DELACORTE PRESS

Text copyright © 2019 by Andrew Prentice
Jacket art copyright © 2019 by Alexander Jansson

All rights reserved. Published in the United States by Delacorte Press,
an imprint of Random House Children's Books,
a division of Penguin Random House LLC, New York.

Delacorte Press is a registered trademark and the colophon is a trademark
of Penguin Random House LLC.

rhcbooks.com

Educators and librarians, for a variety of teaching tools, visit us at RHTeachersLibrarians.com

Library of Congress Cataloging-in-Publication Data is available upon request.
ISBN 978-0-525-64393-7 (trade) — ISBN 978-0-525-64396-8 (lib. bdg.) —
ISBN 978-0-525-64394-4 (ebook)

The text of this book is set in 13.5-point Fournier MT.
Interior design by Ken Crossland

Printed in the United States of America
10 9 8 7 6 5 4 3 2 1
First Edition

Random House Children's Books supports the First Amendment
and celebrates the right to read.

To my brother and sisters:
you are all awesome and I love you.

CHAPTER

1

"Hold tight, Mr. Jenkinson," Oscar Grimstone said. "I'm just going to lean in a bit here. Don't mind me."

Mr. Jenkinson made no reply. But then, his mouth was sewn shut with tiny, invisible stitches, so he couldn't have complained even if he wasn't dead.

Oscar carefully slipped the bow tie around the man's neck.

He caught a strong whiff of porridge as he did it. That was normal. Before Oscar's mum sewed her clients' mouths closed, she always tucked in a few bags of oats to plump up their cheeks. It was one of her secrets.

"Nice floppy knot . . ." Oscar's fingers twirled nimbly. "We don't want it to look like a clip-on, do we?"

She had loads of little secrets, his mum. Odd things happened to a body after it died, and it took even odder things to make it seem like they hadn't.

What we do is an art, she liked to say. *Don't you forget it, Oscar.*

Oscar didn't need convincing. Leaky, stinky stiffs were carried in the back door and peaceful dreamers went out the front to the graveyard. He knew undertaking was magic.

"How does that feel for you, Mr. Jenkinson?" Oscar cocked his head to one side, admiring his handiwork.

Again, Mr. Jenkinson kept up his poker face—but Oscar was sure that if his client could talk he'd be delighted. The bow tie was perfect. The cuffs were perfectly ironed, the hands folded and dusted with talcum powder. You could only faintly make out the smell of embalming chemicals, which Oscar pumped into Mr. Jenkinson to keep his body fresh, just like with Egyptian mummies. A few spritzes of aftershave did the trick. He'd done a fine job.

"Very dapper. You know, loads of your family are coming to see you on your big day, plus half the town. Popular guy." Oscar glanced at the grinning picture of the living Mr. Jenkinson as he picked up a comb. "And you wore a side part, right?"

Carefully, because dead people's skin had a nasty habit of peeling off if you tugged it too hard, he began to comb Mr. Jenkinson's hair.

Oscar was fully aware that twelve-year-old boys aren't often found chatting away with corpses, or combing their hair, but truth be told, Oscar was at his best around the dead. Secretly, he preferred them to living people. They didn't ask awkward questions or say he smelled of bleach. They were good listeners.

And dead people also talked, so long as you knew the right way to look. You could tell a lot about a person from their corpse.

Take Mr. Jenkinson: Oscar knew that he'd smoked at least thirty cigarettes a day, because he'd seen the yellow stains on his fingers. He knew that he'd smiled a lot, because when he was doing his makeup, the deepest wrinkles were the laugh lines around his eyes. He knew from the tattoo Mr. Jenkinson had over his heart that he'd once loved a girl named Mabel very much.

Oscar wondered if Mr. Jenkinson had met up with Mabel wherever he'd gone.

"One last touch and then you're ready." Oscar took a deep breath as he glanced at the vase of lilies by the door.

He'd been dreading this moment. He reached for his crutch, which was leaning against the wall beneath a framed photo of his dad. *You can do it, Oscar,* his father's voice seemed to say. Oscar limped across the room, ignoring the dull pain that always cramped up his leg if he stood in one spot for too long.

He couldn't keep his fingers from trembling a little as he snatched up the largest flower. He cut it down for size, nearly nicking his fingers he went so fast. Then he scuttled back toward the corpse, moving as fast as his bad leg permitted.

But he wasn't fast enough. Just before he got to Mr. Jenkinson, the flower withered. The petals turned black and fell to the floor.

"No," Oscar hissed. "Not again."

"Osky? Are you finished, love?" His mum poked her head around the door. "I'm just going down to the shops—will you . . ." She narrowed her eyes. "What are you hiding behind your back?"

"Nothing, Mum," Oscar lied. He kicked the petals under the table. The dead flower was scrunched up in his fist.

Oscar didn't want her to know.

He didn't want anyone to know about the Curse, which was what he'd started calling it. Problem was, people were starting to notice, especially at school.

When it was his turn to feed the class's tropical fish, he'd sprinkled some flakes into the tank. The next thing he knew, Jerry the clown fish was bobbing on the surface, white belly up. Nobody felt worse for poor Jerry than Oscar, but after that, Gary Stevens started whispering about how he'd poisoned him. The whispers spread quickly.

That was nothing compared to what had happened in the last PE lesson before the end of the year. They always made him goalie—because of his leg, he couldn't run. But this time every blade of grass around him had withered and died. It looked like he'd sprayed a big circle of weed killer on the penalty spot. Then the whispers became taunts. As usual, Gary Stevens and his goons were the worst. They sneered at him every time they passed in the hallways.

Killer boy. Ghoul. Freak.

Gary Stevens started saying that the people in his morgue weren't dead when they went in but died when they looked at Oscar.

It was a good thing it was summer.

"You really shouldn't spend so much time down here," his mum said. She looked worried. "Why don't you go out for some fresh air?"

"But I like it down here," Oscar said.

For a moment, his mum looked like she wanted to argue; then she smiled.

"All right. In an hour, we've got another client coming. That's two in a day!"

"That's good, Mum," Oscar said. He shoved the dead flower stem in his pocket when she wasn't looking.

"I know. It's been so slow! I swear people have just *stopped* dying. Really, it's the strangest thing. Usually July's a good month." Her smile slipped a little. "Now, if people are going to see you, could you do your poor mum a favor and change into something a little *cheerier*? It really helps put clients at ease if you don't look like a vampire, Osk."

"*Mum!*" Just like every other day, Oscar was wearing

the clothes that made him feel most comfortable. Black T-shirt. Black jeans. Black boots. These perfectly matched his black eyes and his jet-black hair. He even had on black socks.

"Please, Osk! We *really* need this job. See, I've bought you a new shirt."

Oscar took the plastic bag she offered. Inside he found a sensible yellow shirt with a starched collar.

He held it up to his chest. "You think they'll prefer this? *Really?*"

"It fits and I like it," his mum said. *"Cheery."*

Oscar raised an eyebrow but didn't argue. Mum had been so worried recently about the business and Oscar locking himself away indoors all summer. He only had to wear the shirt for a meeting, and it would make her happy.

"Good. You put that on," she said. "And I'm off to the butcher's. I'm getting sausages. We are celebrating tonight!"

Oscar heard the front door slam. He slipped off his T-shirt and shivered as goose pimples puckered up his back. They had to keep the temperature barely above freezing in the mortuary. Corpses and summer heat did not mix well.

He dragged the shirt over his head without unbuttoning it. That was a mistake. Something, somewhere, snagged. Now he was blind and his arms were stuck over his head.

Oscar was just thinking how lucky it was that no one could see him, when he heard two soft scratches echo through the room. At the same time, he felt a chill of icy dread spread through him

"Hello?" Oscar said. The shirt was still stuck over his head.

There was another scratchy, skittering noise.

Something was very wrong here. Something horrible. His blood felt cold.

"Who's there?" Oscar shouted. No answer. He was still stuck in the stupid shirt. He backed away blindly and banged into a body cart. Dishes and metal trays crashed on the floor.

Desperate, Oscar grabbed the collar and ripped. The top few buttons tore off their thread.

Oscar blinked. Five scalpels kept in a tray in the corner of the room were hovering in midair just above Mr. Jenkinson.

Oscar was too frightened to scream. The dead man's eyes and mouth were sewn shut, but wispy tendrils of silver fog were leaking through them, and curling across his skin. The fog seemed to be holding the knives up in the air.

Without warning the knives flew at Oscar's head. Oscar threw himself to the ground just in time. The knives smashed into the wall behind him.

The mist was everywhere, twining around the cart holding Mr. Jenkinson, which was rolling toward him. Oscar
yanked the shirt off his back to free himself. Then he dived
out of the way again, ignoring the shooting pain in his bad
leg. Mr. Jenkinson sailed past and crashed into the wall beneath the knives.

"Help!" Oscar shouted, but no one could hear him. A
low, rumbling roar made him whip around just as a huge,
heavy tank of embalming fluid was flying down the narrow
passage between the wall and the row of spare carts.

Oscar rolled to the side. But as he tried to sit up to make
a run for it, he was struck straight in the head. Blinding
stars filled his eyes.

Something rubbery wrapped itself around his throat. It
was horribly strong. It *squeezed*.

Oscar choked, trying to breathe. He looked down and
saw that the hose from the embalming tank had wrapped
itself around his neck like a snake. The silver mist slithered
all over the hose, up toward his jaw, like it knew what it was
doing. Like it wanted Oscar. It scratched across his skin
like a freezing burn.

Oscar began to kick his feet wildly, trying to smash the
tank, but the hose was iron strong and it was crushing the
life from him. Oscar tried to scream, but he couldn't even
breathe. Then a bright, flashing light burst behind his eyes.
The mist filled his vision. His head was roaring. The last

thing he saw was the picture of his father on the wall. Smiling. *Let me go,* Oscar thought. *LET ME GO!*

And as Oscar said it, a switch flicked inside him.

Oscar dropped free. It was a miracle. For a heartbeat, Oscar looked up in utter astonishment as the snakelike hose snapped shut over empty air.

How did I get out of that?

Oscar sprinted for the door, his terror driving him faster than he'd ever run before. He reached out to open it.

But his hand drifted straight through the handle. He toppled forward through the door, landing in the corridor.

Most of Oscar's panicking brain was telling him he needed to get out of here RIGHT NOW. But a small voice was trying very hard to get all these bewildering events in order. A big question was: *How did I just fall through solid wood?*

As he went to push himself to his feet, he saw his hands and realized the answer.

Because his hands weren't there anymore. Or rather, they were only half there.

His fingers seemed to be made of the same shimmery see-through fog he'd seen curling out of Mr. Jenkinson. Panicking, he looked at the rest of his body, but the rest of him was fog too. When he stood up, he could even see the floor through his shoes.

The shock was so powerful that for a brief moment

his mind went blank. He closed his eyes. When he opened them again, he saw that his hands had reappeared and his jeans were black again.

He could also hear a regular thudding noise. It sounded like the embalming tank didn't know how to open a door.

Oscar didn't want to wait for it to find out. He jumped to his feet—and fell back down straightaway. Gasping, with the thudding noise chasing him down the corridor, Oscar dragged himself along the wall to the door, where he grabbed the spare crutch in the umbrella stand.

He burst into the street. He didn't care that he was shirtless. He needed to get away as fast as he could. *I need to warn Mum!*

As he ran, he glanced over his shoulder. No objects were flying at him, which was good, but out of the corner of his eye, he caught a glimpse of something that might have been worse.

A figure was watching him. It was standing in the shadowy alley that ran down the side of his house. A wide-brimmed hat shaded its eyes, and something like a bandanna covered the lower part of its face. As Oscar looked at the figure properly, he realized it seemed to be shimmering.

Then it was gone.

CHAPTER

2

"You could've just told me you didn't want to wear that shirt," Oscar's mum said. "It wasn't cheap, you know."

"I'm telling you the truth, Mum! The . . . the . . ." Oscar flailed an arm at Mr. Jenkinson. "Everything attacked when I was putting it on! I had to rip it off. It was this poltergeist! He had a hat, and I think he was controlling the mist!"

It was bad enough that everything was back to normal. Mr. Jenkinson was lying on the slab with his hands neatly folded over his chest, like there had never been a magical mist that seeped out of him. Even his makeup hadn't smudged—although Oscar was pretty sure his hair used to be parted on the other side.

All the other objects in the room had returned to where they were meant to be, as if they hadn't tried to murder Oscar.

He wasn't *that* sure, though. In fact, Oscar was worried he was losing his mind. He glared at the hose, trying to figure out how it came alive. He almost wanted it to rise again just to prove he wasn't lying.

"Oh, Oscar . . . ," she sighed, chucking scraps of shirt in the bin. "Come on. . . . Let's go to the kitchen. Have a cup of tea. You'll feel better."

His mum's solution to every crisis was tea. Oscar suspected that if a crazed man-eating lion charged her, her first thought would be to ask if it wanted one lump of sugar or two. She took four this time, which meant she probably thought the apocalypse was coming.

"What are people going to *say*, Osk? Running about town like a naked maniac! You looked completely crazy. That gossipy butcher will have a nice story to tell, and you can be sure that he'll tell *everyone*."

"People aren't interested in me, Mum."

"It matters, Osk. Who's going to bring their dead granny here if they think we're the sort of people who buy sausages half-naked! Undertaking is the most serious business there is."

"I'm sorry," Oscar said.

"No! I'm sorry. It's not right for a boy to spend all summer with dead people. Especially if he's . . ." His mum stopped herself. She took a deep glug of tea.

"If he's *what*?" Oscar said.

"I was . . . I was just going to say . . ." She sipped her tea again. She didn't want to meet his eye.

"Let me guess. You wanted to say 'especially if he's already odd.'"

His mum didn't look up.

"Why don't you just say it? Maybe I am. But so what? I can't change, Mum."

Mrs. Grimstone smiled sadly. "I don't want you to change, Osk. You know I didn't mean that. It's just after the accident the doctors said I had to watch out for signs. It was an awful bump you took."

"But, Mum! I'M. NOT. SEEING. THINGS!"

Oscar had never shouted at his mum like that. His mom's knuckles went white as she gripped her cup in front of her, like a shield. Then she spoke quietly and fast. "Love, I think you should go and see a doctor. A proper one. They'll help you—and it'll get you out of the house. . . ."

Oscar hadn't drunk a sip of his tea, but he stormed up to his bedroom.

It was almost midnight before Oscar calmed down. He hadn't left his room and had missed dinner, even though he was hungry and the sausages smelled delicious. He lay in his bed staring into the dark.

His mum thought he was going crazy.

There was nothing wrong with him. His head was fine.

Well, maybe his neck was still aching a bit where the tank had nailed him. But that was just the proof he needed to know he hadn't imagined it all.

And it definitely wasn't anything to do with the accident either. His leg had been shattered in five places in the car crash that killed his dad, but there was no damage to his brain. Anyway, that was *years* ago, when he was a baby. He'd never seen anything like that mist in all his life.

Actually, Oscar thought, *that isn't true.* The dead clown fish and the poisoned grass were real and weird, not to mention all the dead flowers. . . .

Maybe it's good she didn't believe me, Oscar told himself. Suddenly, he felt relieved. She didn't know about the other stuff. Which was good.

This was the scariest thought. What if it was all his fault? What if his Curse had made the corpse come alive? Maybe it was all linked.

It was too horrible to think about—and that was just the problem. Oscar realized that he hadn't really been thinking properly at all. He'd been ignoring everything, hoping it was going to go away. And now it seemed to be getting worse.

What if it got really bad?

What if he hugged his mum and she died?

The thought was interrupted by a sudden chill of icy

dread running down his spine. It was exactly the same feeling he'd had in the morgue, as Mr. Jenkinson attacked. Oscar's heart thudded as the tingling cold crept through his body.

He remembered the shimmering figure in the hat that he'd seen standing outside his house. The ghost.

Maybe that thing had come back?

The curtains in his room fluttered gently. He switched on his lamp and limped across the room to shut the window. His fingers reached for the curtain, and slowly, he inched them open.

Marigold Street looked as normal as ever. Sleepy houses, parked cars, neatly trimmed hedges.

Across the road, Gary Stevens, Oscar's nemesis and neighbor, was walking his dog. His new dog. The other one had died recently. Gary had blamed Oscar even though he had nothing to do with it.

The new dog seemed to have spotted something. It was tugging at its leash and growling.

Oscar just had time to wonder why, when he was blinded by a bright flash of light.

When he could see again, a shimmering green carriage was rolling down the road, drawn by two rake-thin horses. The carriage lurched up onto the pavement. It was heading right for Gary!

"Watch ou—"

The cry caught in Oscar's throat as he saw the carriage roll right *through* Gary and his dog, which barked madly. Gary didn't appear to have noticed at all. The carriage continued, rattling through cars and lampposts as if they weren't there.

"What's going on?" Oscar murmured.

The carriage drew to a sharp halt outside Oscar's house.

The dread froze inside him.

Oscar stopped breathing. As he looked down, he realized the horses weren't just thin. They were actually skeletons, with flickering ghost bodies.

This was bad.

Maybe the ghost had come back to finish the job? Oscar imagined the dead bodies slowly sitting up in the morgue, standing, and with blind eyes climbing the stairs to murder his mother in her bed.

Oscar turned for the door to warn her, just as two ghostly figures jumped down from the cart. The first pulled an apple and a carrot from her pocket.

Oscar blinked. This wasn't what he was expecting.

The girl ghost gave the snacks to the horses.

Oscar blinked again.

She was a girl about Oscar's age, dressed in very old-fashioned lacy clothes. She wasn't a skeleton, although she shimmered just like the horses. She pulled an object from her belt and squinted at it.

The other figure was tall and thin. Oscar couldn't tell if he was a skeleton or not because he was completely encased inside a full suit of plate armor.

Both of them wore little silver shields on their chests like sheriff badges. As they walked closer, Oscar saw the thing in the girl's hand. It looked like a wooden hair dryer. She was shaking it, as if it wasn't working.

The knight gave the hair dryer a whack with his metal fist. That seemed to do the trick because the girl held it up and pointed it at Oscar's house. She muttered something under her breath.

Carefully, Oscar bent down to the opening in the window to hear what she was saying.

"Heaps of phantasma coming from here . . ." The girl's voice. "Illegal use of poltergeisting including corpse animation . . . Fifth-level breach at least."

The knight's reply was muffled under his visor.

"Right! It's a very powerful signal. Haunt me sideways! And I thought the Monday shift was supposed to be quiet."

Shifts? Signals? What are they talking about? Quickly Oscar's fear slipped away as a fierce curiosity surged up in its place. He had to find out what was going on.

The two figures walked right up to Oscar's front door and stepped through it.

Oscar crept across his bedroom and peeked out into the hallway. The house was dark. There was no sign of the two visitors. He couldn't hear anything except for the rasping snores of his mum from along the corridor.

He grabbed his crutch and snuck down the stairs.

His heart was hammering like a piston by the time he reached the mortuary door. He still couldn't hear anything. The two figures (if they were in there) were moving silently.

He put his ear to the wood.

"Good gracious!" That was the girl's voice.

Oscar froze.

"I'm picking up a very strong source of phantasma! This is incredible! Look at the dial. It's whizzing!"

The knight grunted something.

"Not from in here, though. It's . . ."

Before Oscar had time to react, the two ghosts stepped through the wall, almost on top of him.

". . . out there," the girl finished.

It was hard to say who was more surprised. They all goggled at one another. The two ghosts were easier to notice close-up, even though they were still see-through. The girl was dressed in Victorian clothes: long skirt, hat, high collar. She had a young face but old, watchful eyes. The knight had a mean-looking sword strapped to his belt. His hand was on the pommel.

"Cedric. I reckon he can see us!" the girl said.

The knight lifted the visor above his mouth. "Poppy-cock!" he whined in a nasal voice. "It can't be!"

"Course I can see you," Oscar said. "What's going on?"

"He can hear us too. What *is* going on?" the girl asked. "How many fingers am I holding up?"

"Three," Oscar said.

Her frown deepened. "How's he doing that?"

She pointed her wooden hair dryer at Oscar and waved it around.

The knight snorted in surprise. "I say!" There was a dial on the back of the device. Oscar could just see the needle swinging wildly about.

"Look at those readings," the girl said. "Truly *exceptional* concentrations of phantasma."

"What's flantansma?" Oscar asked.

"*Phantasma*. Ghost essence, my boy," the knight said.

The girl was frowning. "And you're bones so you shouldn't have any of it."

"*Bones?*"

The girl sighed. "This phantasmagraph thinks you're a ghost. No bones. But you're clearly living—bones. Easy enough to understand?"

"No," Oscar said. "It's not."

"Try punching yourself in the head."

"What? No!"

"Suit yourself." The girl grinned and turned away.

"Wait, please!" Oscar had so many questions they were burning in his mind. Why were they here? Why was he filled with ghost essence? Were he and his mum in danger?

The girl tapped her foot with impatience. "Yes?"

Oscar's face twisted with the effort of understanding. "I think you're ghosts, am I right?"

"Correct. My name is Sally Cromarty, and this is my partner, Sir Cedric Bosanquet."

"Oscar Grimstone."

The knight gave a slight nod. "Remarkable." He slipped back through the wall.

"Why . . . why have you come to my house?"

"Oscar, we are detectives employed by the Ministry of Ghosts." Sally tapped the silver shield on her chest. The letters *GLE* were stamped into it. "Ghost Law Enforcement. We came out here to investigate a suspected case of illegal corpse animation—and what do we find? A glorious mess, that's what. *You* won't remember any of this. The only ones who need to worry are me and Cedric. Mess always means paperwork. Mounds of it."

The knight moaned.

"I know, Cedric!" the girl snapped. "I say we do a quick

sweep, then head back to the shop. We can send forensics and a wipe team later. They can deal with Grimbone."

"Grim-*stone*! And I don't need dealing with!" Oscar didn't like the sound of a wipe team.

"Don't worry. It's quite standard procedure. They'll just fix your memory. Perfectly painless and you won't remember anything. Much better. You'll see."

"But I don't want you to fix my memory! I want to know what's going on."

"That's not going to happen, sir. This is ghost business, and you're . . . Well, I'm not sure what you are, exactly."

"Right. That's why you've got to help me! An embalming tank attacked me! Knives too." Oscar almost mentioned his Curse but held back. What would they think of him if they knew he made things die?

"You were attacked by a tank?"

"Yes! It came alive. There was this strange mist."

The knight poked his head through the door. "Not a ghoul! I've detected no necromancy here. Only a powerful reanimation. Must have used a barrelful of phantas—"

"I'm telling the truth. Stuff kept attacking me—and I think it was because of a ghost in a hat."

"What kind of hat?" Sally asked.

"It was sort of a wide one. I didn't get that good a look, though."

The girl was interested. He could tell by the way her eyes widened. The knight leaned closer, examining Oscar through a sort of fold-out telescope with knobs and dials all over it.

"You didn't get a look at his face?" Sally asked.

"No, I couldn't see. I think it was wearing something like a bandanna over its mouth as well. . . . *Please*. You have to help us. The person could come back. Don't you want to know what's going on? If you wipe my memory, you will have lost a witness!"

The knight jabbed the telescope at Oscar. "The young fellow's right about that."

"I know, Cedric! Golly!" Sally said before muttering something under her breath. "But we can't take him with us. It's against the law."

"No! I mean . . . Yes, you have to take me!" Oscar pleaded. "Good idea."

Sally was peeling him apart with her gray eyes. It was impossible to tell what she was thinking. It was also quite frightening.

"Well?" Oscar asked.

"What a bleeding *mess*!" Sally snapped. "And no. Even if I wanted to, you can't. You're a fleshy, see."

She reached out to touch him. Her hand passed through his shoulder. Oscar felt a cold tingling where her fingers had brushed him.

"Ghost things and living things don't belong together. Where we're going, you can't come." She turned to Cedric. "You finished in there?"

The knight nodded. "Yeah."

"Smart work," Sally said. "So. Goodbye, Oscar. I'd like you to know that all will be well. It will be as if this never happened."

She nodded briskly; then both ghosts floated away down the corridor and disappeared through the front door.

CHAPTER

3

Oscar clenched his fists as he stared after the two ghosts. He couldn't believe they were leaving him like this, with so many questions. His eyes fell on the photograph of his father hanging on the wall.

It was his favorite picture. The last one taken of his dad before the accident. Oscar was in it, playing with a toy car. His dad was grinning down at him. He looked very proud. And then Oscar had a remarkable thought. Maybe his dad was a ghost too.

Could he find him? *Speak* to him? Oscar had imagined his dad's voice in his head a million times—he'd love to hear it again, just once. . . .

Oscar burst out of the front door as fast as his crutch could carry him.

The carriage was already turning around in the street. The two ghost detectives had climbed up into their seats.

"Stop!" Oscar shouted, leaping in front of the carriage. The terrifying skeleton horses loomed over him.

"Please don't make a scene, sir," Sally said.

"But I want to know if I can talk to my dad! He could be a ghost too."

Sally seemed to look at him with a flicker of pity for a second. "No. Against the rules."

"I'm not moving."

"Suit yourself."

The knight flicked the reins, and the skeleton horses walked forward. Both of them snorted at Oscar as they marched right through him, sending a wave of ice through his body. Their translucent bones gleamed silvery green. Bits of withered flesh still clung to them here and there like badly chewed chicken drumsticks.

Oscar tried grabbing the carriage to pull himself up, but his hand went straight through the wood, making it tingle.

The carriage kept rolling off. The detectives' legs passed through his shoulders and head. Now his chest was poking through the bed of the carriage, the boards flowing around him as if Oscar was a rock standing in a fast-flowing stream. "Stop!" he pleaded. He could just make out his feet through the transparent planks. The sheer oddness reminded him of before, when he'd turned invisible and fallen from Mr. Jenkinson's grip.

The carriage finished passing through him, and Oscar

turned to watch his last chance to get some answers—to speak to his dad!—rolling faster and faster away down the street. The hope that had burned so brightly for a moment flickered out.

He was so desperate that he almost didn't notice the change that had come over him.

Oscar looked down at his shimmering hands. They were see-through.

So were his legs. His arms. His feet.

For the second time that day, without quite knowing how he'd done it, Oscar Grimstone had become a ghost.

"Hold up!"

Oscar didn't wait to wonder how it had happened. He was already running after the carriage, making no footprints in the mud. Around him, Oscar noticed that the houses and bushes and cars appeared dulled, like he was viewing them through sunglasses. But as everything darkened, the ghosts and their carriage sparkled brighter, like they were made of pure moonlight.

Oscar pumped his ghost legs. Then he was *floating*, his wheeling feet only faintly brushing the ground.

A huge grin spread on Oscar's face as he moved faster toward the carriage.

His crutch had turned ghostly too, but now he didn't need it because his legs were awesome! He dropped it in the road. The crutch snapped back to normal as soon it left his hand. It clattered on the asphalt.

"Stop!" Oscar shouted, but the skeleton horses accelerated.

That didn't matter. He took three great, bounding strides and jumped straight into the back of the carriage.

He landed with a thump on the same boards that had flowed about him seconds before. The two detectives were staring at him openmouthed.

"You look like you've seen a ghost," Oscar said.

"By Mortis's beard!" Sally gasped.

Cedric opened up the lower half of his visor. "Stab me with an otter! That's mighty impressive."

"A human turning into a ghost?!" Sally yelled, grinning from ear to ear. "You've even frightened the horses."

"So can I come with you?" Oscar asked.

The detectives glanced at each other. "Fine," Sally said. "Got a few more questions myself."

"Thank you," Oscar said. The thought suddenly crossed his mind that it might be quite dangerous, being taken to the world of the dead. "Er . . . I mean, if I'll be back in time for breakfast? It's just, my mum will worry if not."

"Certainly," Sir Cedric said. "You have my word."

"Right, that's settled." Sally nodded. "You ready? Next stop, headquarters."

Sir Cedric shook the reins, and the carriage sped off down the road. There was no wind even though they were traveling fast. No sound either; but a mist soon spread out of nowhere. "Hold on!" Sally shouted. "You might not like this."

Almost at once, the mist was so thick that Oscar couldn't see his hand in front of his face.

The carriage drove on through the fog faster and faster. They'd left Marigold Street, the whole of Little Worthington in fact, far behind. Oscar knew this, even though he couldn't say how he was sure. Dark spindly shapes whirled past them like huge grasping hands. Sir Cedric muttered something to Sally.

"Where are we?" Oscar asked.

"The void!" Sally yelled. "And these are void horses, descended from the steeds of the Valkyries. They run so quick they can break the phantasmic barrier. That's why they need to be bony! Can't have any extra weight."

"Right," Oscar said. None of it sounded very reassuring.

"Whoooah!" Sir Cedric pulled up hard on the reins.

There was a bright flash. The fog cleared.

They were on a busy road, lights glaring out from bars, late-night stores, and high office buildings—some ancient, some made of glass, reaching high overhead.

Is this . . . London? Oscar wondered. *That's fifty miles away!*

A pair of bright headlights blazed down on them. Sir Cedric didn't flinch or steer away.

It was a bus! A big red London bus and it was coming straight for them. Oscar screamed as the light filled his vision. He continued screaming as they drove on through it. The driver and then the passengers sitting in their seats flashed past him. None of the passengers looked up from their phones.

Oscar was crouched in the bottom of the cart with his hands over his eyes.

"You'll get used to it," Sally said. She was chuckling.

They drove straight through another bus, then streams of cars and other vehicles. Oscar managed not to cry out but couldn't stop himself flinching each time. To distract himself, he tried to look about him.

"Where are we?"

"Fleet Street," Sally answered. "Pretty good driving, Sir C—it's hard to be accurate in the void."

Then all pitched forward as Sir Cedric grunted and jerked on the reins. The cart stopped hard, the horses rearing up.

"Blimey!" shouted Sally down to someone in the road. "You watch yourself!"

They'd narrowly avoided hitting a child. A small, shimmering child who'd run out into the street from a tavern to chase a flickering ball. Its mother came running out and picked up the crying little boy. She waved her thanks to Sir Cedric.

"Ought to know better, Francine!" Sally cried as the cart moved off. "You've only had four hundred years to teach that child to mind a road!"

"Is she a ghost?" Oscar asked.

"Both of them are. Francine works at the Ancient Mariner inn—best jellied eels in Londinium. They both died in the Great Plague as I recall. Snagged a watching visa to look after her family and they're still hanging about. Not ready to let go of the living world. Happens sometimes. People stick around for a whole host of reasons. Sir C, for example, he just couldn't give up on the living world."

"That's right," the knight grunted.

"Some ghosts have a skill they've mastered—and they just want to keep doing it forever. They've a passion, see? Others get offered a job at the Ministry. . . ."

"Is that what happened to you?" Oscar asked.

"No. I had . . . *unfinished business*." A dark gleam appeared in Sally's eye.

"Wait! So are there lots of ghosts, then?" Oscar asked, still desperately trying to keep up.

"Why don't you see for yourself?" Sally smirked.

Oscar looked out the carriage window, and his mouth dropped open in astonishment.

"Wha . . . whah . . ."

The usual houses and cars and living pedestrians were there—but they all seemed a bit faded and gray. Moving amongst them, and shining brightly, were dozens of shimmering people dressed in all kinds of historic clothing—some had ruffles and flamboyant waistcoats, another man wore a vintage pin-striped suit and fedora, and a woman in an old-fashioned sari was buying a newspaper from a scruffy urchin on a street corner. The dead seemed more real than the living.

"Why haven't I seen any of this before?" Oscar whispered.

Sally shrugged. "Maybe you just didn't look properly."

"That mist did something to me."

There were shining ghost buildings too, crammed in the gaps between real houses—or even on top of them. They came in all types. Mud huts, ancient wooden houses, drunken, half-timbered mansions leaning out over the street. They had doors in strange places, and the ghosts were moving in and out of them as if they lived there.

They did, presumably.

Oscar was suddenly struck by how very, very old the city was. So many people had died here. So many houses had burned down, or fallen apart, or simply been built over.

But it hadn't gone away. Nothing went away, it seemed. "This is amazing!" Oscar said.

Sally nodded. "You'd be surprised what goes on under your nose, eh? Londinium, a city of ghosts, right on top of the living city. And much more interesting, if you ask me."

She was right. What if his dad was here? The thought was almost too exciting to grab hold of. His dad! He might actually see him again.

"Does my dad live here?" Oscar asked.

"We can look him up," Sir Cedric said. "He'll be on the record."

Oscar couldn't believe any of this. How did it all work? What would he say to his dad if he found him? How would he explain this to Mum?

He stretched his bad leg like he always did when he was confused.

But that ended up being a big mistake.

The cold, tingly feeling inside him disappeared, and Oscar turned real and solid. He fell through the cart, thumping down into the road. Pain jolted through his bad leg. The horse and cart trotted away in front of him. Sally's head was craned out the side, her wide eyes fixed on him with utter astonishment.

Around him, the living world had turned back to full color. The noises of car horns and rushing traffic became loud, and Oscar realized that in his ghost form the sounds of the living world had been muted too. Oscar could still see the ghosts, though they had lost some of their shimmering moonlit quality.

"Blimey," said a bearded ghost wearing a cravat, turning from a line at a fruit stall to stare at Oscar.

The fruit vendor, a large woman in an apron, gawked. "Did that ghost just turn into a fleshy?"

"Won't be a fleshy for much longer," a thin woman in a ball gown said, looking past Oscar.

A horn blared in Oscar's ears. His head snapped round, and he was blinded by headlights. Two tons of black taxi skidded toward him. The taxi driver swerved to the right and crashed into a lamppost. A bicyclist smashed into the taxi and went somersaulting over his handlebars.

He landed beside Oscar.

A crowd gathered. Ghosts and people. The humans had no idea ghosts moved around them. Now Oscar was in his human form, the living regained their color and pointed at him, some taking out their phones to record videos.

". . . just appeared from thin air, I swear!"

". . . almost got hit!"

The taxi driver was screaming at Oscar. The bicyclist was screaming at the taxi driver. Sally was screaming too, but only Oscar and the ghosts could hear her.

"You idiot!" she yelled. "Do you have any idea how much trouble you're making? Turn back into a ghost right *now*!"

The cart had rolled on ten paces without him.

"Um . . . ah . . ."

It was impossible. He could feel all the people staring at him. His bad leg hurt where he'd landed awkwardly.

"I don't know how," Oscar said.

"You what?" the taxi driver growled.

"Just think!" Sally shouted.

But it was hard to think—with all those eyes and all that noise and confusion whirling around. The taxi driver and the cyclist were standing nose to nose and looked like they were about to fight.

Oscar shut his eyes.

"What are you doing, you idiot! Hurry up!" Sally yelled.

The first time he'd done it, he'd seen the picture of his dad. That was when he changed.

The second time he'd been slipping through the cart, and then he'd thought about his dad and then . . .

Oscar pictured his dad in his head. It wasn't hard. He'd stared at that particular photo so many times. He knew every detail of it. His dad's little bald spot. The faint smile on his lips. The careful way he was holding the little boy in his lap—as if he would never let anything bad happen to him.

"You can do it, Oscar."

Oscar vanished.

"Thank Mortis! You didn't look like you knew how to turn back." Sally chuckled.

"Don't do that again," Sir Cedric said. "This is a level-three breach."

"Three?" Sally shook her head. "There's more than thirty people who've seen him. It's a four at least! You're more trouble than a train full of soul feeders, Oscar."

"You're too much paperwork," Sir Cedric grumbled. Then he stiffened, like a dog catching a scent. "Hear that?"

A wailing screech of a siren was coming closer and closer.

"Uh-oh," Sally said. "Here comes the awkward squad."

The siren was getting louder.

"Who are they?" Oscar asked. "They don't sound good."

"They're not. They're the wipers," Sally started. "They'll make sure no one remembers this little accident." She cocked her head to one side. "Course, not sure what they'll do about you. Me? I'd want you to talk, but the wipers do like everything to be tidy. And you're a mess."

"I'm not a mess! I'm in danger," Oscar pleaded. "My *mum's* in danger. There was a ghost that attacked our mortuary. And I can meet my dad! I haven't seen him since I was tiny. I need to find out what's going on. Please don't let them wipe me!"

Sally and Sir Cedric exchanged a look. Because of his helmet, it was hard to tell what the knight was thinking, but Sally's eyes widened.

Oscar was worried too. If his memory got wiped, he'd forget all this amazing new stuff.

Worse, he'd never meet his dad.

CHAPTER 4

Oscar didn't wait for the wipers to find him. He jumped from the carriage and ran off down the nearest alley.

His new legs worked like magic, and he just went, picking up speed until his toes were barely brushing the paving slabs. Left. A right. He was hurtling—but now his path was blocked by a crowd of tourists, arguing over a map.

"Get out of the way!" Oscar shouted.

The other ghosts moved, but the humans didn't even look up.

"WATCHIT!" Just as he was about to smash into the pack like a bowling ball, Oscar remembered that he was a ghost, and they wouldn't be able to hear him.

They couldn't stop him either. Oscar zipped right through the tourists' bodies without breaking stride. They didn't notice a thing, though it felt a bit funny to run right through living people. Oscar got a little shiver, a scrap of thought, from each one. The last man was thinking about cabbages.

"Hoy! Come back here, you rascal!" Sir Cedric roared.

Oscar glanced over his shoulder and saw Sally and the armored knight tearing through the same crowd of tourists. They were right behind him!

He shouldn't have looked back. Suddenly, a wall was looming in front of him. There was no time to stop. Oscar threw his hands in front of his face, fully expecting to smash his teeth and smear his nose flat on the hard brick.

Instead, he felt nothing. He surged through the wall into an empty office full of desks and computers.

Nothing could stop him! Oscar let out a wild whoop as he charged on. He didn't stop for doors, or water coolers, or photocopiers. He didn't stop when he ran straight from one building into another. He didn't stop when the floor suddenly disappeared and he found he was running on empty air over a busy street.

As he sprinted on, he sank gradually back toward the ground, treading down through the air. He was aware that behind him, Sally and Sir Cedric were still chasing him, but he was also aware—with a burst of savage glee—that he was running away from them. These fools couldn't keep up with Oscar Grimstone!

Oscar had never run away from anyone in his life. He'd never felt like this either. Before, limping across a room without a crutch would leave him gasping for breath. Now, the pure joy of speed filled him with a golden glow. He wasn't getting tired. He was getting faster.

Funny how it took becoming a ghost to feel alive.

And he wasn't tiring out. As the two ghosts fell farther behind him, Oscar swerved off the road and charged down a narrow passage, ignoring the steep steps with great bounding strides. Ahead of him, the passage opened into a wider space. He could hear the murmur of a large crowd.

Maybe he could lose the two police ghosts in . . .

"Wha . . . ," Oscar moaned.

He came out of the alley and stopped dead. He was on the riverbank. All around him, long lines of ghosts stretched out as far as he could see. Men, women, children, even babies shone brilliantly against the dull gray ordinary world. They were all waiting patiently to board an enormous ship that glowed with the same eerie ghost light. It was the biggest ship Oscar had ever seen—it had three great smokestacks like an old ocean liner out of the movies. Thousands of shivering green lights flickered at its windows.

Something strange had happened to the river too. Oscar hadn't spent much time in London, but he was pretty sure that the Thames couldn't possibly be this wide. He couldn't even see the other side—only a faint, far-off glow just beyond the horizon.

It felt more like he was standing at the edge of a great black ocean.

What was going on?

"Hurry up! Hurry up! Last chance to board for your trip to the Other Side!" An officer in a crisp white uniform with a three-foot-long golden megaphone was roaring orders from the deck. "Keep calm and carry on queuing. We still have manners, even if we're dead."

"There he is!"

Oscar glanced back and saw Sally and Sir Cedric steaming down the passage toward him. He dived into the crowd, pushing through the neat lines. Ghosts groaned as he stepped on their toes and squeezed between them. After he made his way deep into the heart of the crowd, there were more grunts of disapproval, and several hard stares.

"What do you think you're doing?" said the thin-lipped woman who he'd cut in front of. "I've been waiting here for two hours."

"I'm sorry," Oscar said, thinking fast. If she made a scene, he was sure that Sally and Sir Cedric would notice at once. "I just . . . I just saw the *killers* who murdered me. They were back there. I was scared—I wanted to hide."

"Crumbs, I'm sorry, love." The woman's scowl softened. "That's awful. Here take this—that way they won't recognize you."

She shrugged off her large duffle coat.

"Thank you," Oscar said. Gratefully, he huddled deep inside the heavy coat.

"Wait," the lady said. "If they killed *you*, how are they dead as well?"

"Well . . . It was funny." Oscar started thinking of another lie. "They slipped on my blood . . . and *drowned*. That's why they're so angry!"

"Nice one!" the lady said. "Shhh. Heads down. *Here they come.*"

Through a gap in the duffle coat, Oscar saw Sir Cedric's armored feet stomping right by him. He heard Sally calling his name.

"Ooh—those two looked mean! So why did they want to kill you?"

"Um . . . because my father was a . . . a judge, and he sent their brother to prison."

The woman, whose name was Muffy, kept on asking questions, and Oscar's lie kept getting bigger and stranger. It turned out that Muffy had died because she'd choked on a grape.

"It's not nearly as dramatic as being murdered," she sniffed. "The chap from this ministry who collected me found it pretty amusing. Guess I could see the funny side. It's all a bit of fun being dead, isn't it?"

All the time, the lines of ghosts continued to shuffle forward. They actually moved quickly. The officer with the megaphone kept roaring instructions, urging them on and praising the ghosts for staying in an organized line. Oscar still wasn't sure why everyone wanted to board this huge steamship.

As they got closer, Oscar realized—with a jolt of horror—that the ship was actually made of bones.

"Nearly there," said Muffy cheerfully. "I wonder what happens on the Other Side."

Oscar decided he didn't want to find out.

"Thanks for the coat, Muffy," he said. "But there's something important I just remembered. Good luck!"

He tried to sneak away—but he was instantly spotted by Captain Megaphone.

"Hey there! Step back in line!" the officer boomed. "No barging, no cutting!"

Oscar didn't step back in line. He continued walking away, hoping it wasn't him that had been spotted.

It was.

Out of nowhere, two skeleton sailors appeared on either side of him. They grabbed his arms so that he couldn't move. Their ivory-yellow grins were not friendly.

"Excuse me . . . ," one skeleton said, raising his hand to stop him. "Do you happen to have a *visa* to stay in the Living World, *sir*?"

"No, I don't," Oscar said. "But that's all right. I was just on my way to get one."

"Oh, that won't do, sir," the other skeleton said. "If you've been assigned to cross over to the Other Side—that's what you've got to do. You had a chance to apply for living world visas when you filled out the post-death forms. I trust your spirit guide gave you the post-death forms?"

"Yes! I mean . . . No! I just need to—"

"No, you don't, sir. No visa, no sticking around. Let's carry him on board, Bob."

"Right you are, Helen. Up he goes."

As if he weighed nothing, the two skeletons lifted Oscar up by his arms and carried him between the patient rows of ghosts toward the gangway that led up to the ship. There was nothing Oscar could do about it. Their bony fingers were as cold and strong as iron bars.

"Wait!" he shouted. "There's been a mistake."

"We never make mistakes, sir," Helen said, as if this was obvious.

"Perish the thought!" Bob exclaimed. "There hasn't been a mistake for ten thousand years. Not on this ship. Not on our watch. You're ready for the Other Side, my lad, and the *Chiron* will take you."

Now they were carrying him up the gangway itself. The bone ship—the *Chiron*—loomed just ahead. Oscar didn't like the look of it at all. He reached into his pocket, hoping there was something—anything—in there that he could use to escape.

His hands found his phone. For a glorious micro instant, he was comforted by the thought of calling his mum—but that joy was just as quickly snuffed out by the bleak realization that his mum was fifty miles away and had probably forgotten to charge her phone, and even if she hadn't, she'd never believe what was going on.

How would he explain it? Oscar also had grave doubts about whether a ghost phone would have reception.

He was almost at the top of the ramp now. There was no way out. This was it. He was going to the Other Side.

How is this happening to me? I'm not dead. It gave Oscar an idea. He closed his eyes and changed back into human form, and the next thing he knew the skeleton hands lost their grip on him and he was falling through the air.

It was a long drop to the river. The water was cold when Oscar hit it. He plunged deep, and came up in a panic, terrified that he would be trapped under the horrible ghost ship. He saw that the living world had regained its color. The other side of the river had reappeared as well. His bad leg hurt. He tried to kick with his good leg, but the cold dark water was sucking him down.

Oscar was not a strong swimmer at the best of times, so it was a solid piece of luck that he just managed to grab hold of a slime-covered rope and drag himself toward a set of stairs leading down into the water.

An old man was sprawled on the stairs.

"Therza wet cat!" he wheezed as Oscar crawled out of the water, choking and spluttering. "Whatchu night swimming for? Didchu wanna drink? Herhher!"

Oscar was cold and wet—and he didn't feel like being laughed at.

He knew what he needed to do. He thought of his dad: he imagined his smile, what it would be like to see it in real life. Hope coursed through Oscar like blazing fire, and he turned back into a ghost.

The man screamed in terror and ran off into the night.

As soon as he stepped back into the ghost world, the Chiron and the ghostly lines were back. The river had carried him about two hundred yards downstream. He turned to see the Chiron in the distance. There was some kind of commotion still going on back on the gangway—it looked like the officer was shouting at Bob and Helen through his megaphone, but there weren't any ghosts nearby. He'd gotten away!

Oscar was even more pleased when he realized that he was also warm and dry again. Apparently, ghosts can't get wet.

His comfort was short-lived.

"Oscar Grimstone!" Sally's voice roared out of the darkness. "Hold it right there!"

Oscar started running again along the riverbank, away from the Chiron. He zipped past ordinary people and ghosts.

The ghosts gawked at him as he ran past in such a hurry, but none of them tried to stop him.

Sally was not giving up. Each time he looked back she was still there, but maybe just a little bit farther away. There was a grimness in her face that told him she wasn't going to give up this chase easily.

Ahead he saw a grand flickering building towering up beside the river. The building looked busy, with a steady stream of ghosts bustling through its wide doors. Above them, a British flag hung limp from its flagpole. There wasn't much wind in the land of the dead.

Oscar checked behind again. Sally was pretty far back now, only just in sight.

This might be his chance. Oscar ran straight for the doors.

"No running," snapped a security guard as Oscar burst through into an enormous vaulted hall.

Oscar slowed to a brisk walk as he looked for a place to hide. He allowed himself a smile. Hiding wasn't going to be hard, not in this madhouse.

Dozens of desks and cubicles dotted about the hall, and lines of ghosts wound in every direction, crossing and tangling with one another like a crazy spiderweb. Every now and then the room echoed with a heavy *chunk* as an official stamp hammered down on a document. The lines moved very slowly. Oscar supposed the dead had the time to be patient.

It was only when Oscar passed a sign that said *Ghost Visas* that he stopped. Maybe this was where he could find out where his father was now.

"Can I help you, citizen? Direct you somewhere?" A gray-faced official in a pin-striped suit slipped up through the floor, right beside him.

Oscar jumped.

"Are you here for a visa?"

"Yes," Oscar said. "Yes. A visa. That's right."

"Very good," the official said quickly. "Haunting visas over there in lines five, nine, and seventeen. Watching briefs in the far corner. If you're here for a military pass, then you'll need to go to the fourth floor. Ministry recruitment is on the twenty-seven hundred and ninety-second floor. Elevator's broken."

"Thank you," Oscar said, trying to shuffle around so the official was between him and the door—in case Sally barged in at any moment "And if we wanted to trace a ghost? Where would we go?"

"That would be in the Directory on three hundred and thirteen. They are next to the kindergarten."

"Three hundred and thirteen." Oscar nodded. "Right, then. I'd best be getting along."

"Where's your spirit guide, young man?"

"Spirit guide?" Oscar said. "Oh, I left him—"

"*Left him!* This is most irregular. Oh dear . . ."

The official snapped a walkie-talkie out of his sleeve and began mumbling rapidly into it. "We've got an incident. Code Tango Werewolf. Foyer, by the chancery line. I repeat, Code Tango Werewolf!"

He smiled thinly at Oscar. "If you'll just wait with me . . ."

Oscar got ready to run again.

"Don't even *think* about it, Oscar," Sally snapped. She was striding across the hall toward him, holding up her silver badge. "We'll take it from here," she said to the official.

"But this is not your jurisdiction, little girl!" The official puffed up in his pin-striped suit like a frog. "Regulations clearly state that—"

"Little girl!" Sally said through gritted teeth, clearly in no mood for this. "Do you know what this badge is?"

The official suddenly realized who he was dealing with. He gulped.

"If you don't step aside, buffoon, I'll slap you with regulations that'll make you wish you'd never died. In triplicate!"

"*Ghouls!*" the official murmured as he quickly got out of Sally's way. "Of course, Officer, take him if you must!"

Sally grabbed hold of Oscar and dragged him toward

the door. Her grip felt even stronger than the skeleton sailors'.

"Did you see his face?" Sally snorted.

Oscar couldn't believe it. Her whole body was shaking with laughter.

"You're not mad?" he asked.

"Mad?" Sally said, smiling. "Of course not. You're amazing. I can't even fathom how much trouble you've caused. I count three major incidents in one night, three minors, and a potential rolling breach as well. How do you switch back and forth like that?"

They walked together out of the building. Sally was still chuckling.

"Please don't take me home," Oscar pleaded. "Please don't wipe my memory. I need to find out what's going on. I need to find my dad."

"That's the thing." Sally grinned. "You don't have to worry about that from me. If I had you wiped, Oscar, I'd have to explain to someone how I was responsible for letting you cause this mess. And that would be the end of me. I'd be filling in forms for the next millennium. Besides, you're the most interesting thing that's happened round here for a long time."

She gave Oscar another one of her wide grins. No one ever smiled at Oscar like that, and certainly not a girl his own age.

To his surprise, Oscar found himself smiling back. It made his face feel strange. He grinned again, feeling the rusty muscles move beneath his skin.

"What are you so happy about?" Sally asked.

"I work better here," Oscar said. "And it's great."

"Then we better get going." Sally let go of his arm and set off into the city, striding away from the river.

"Where are we going?"

"I'm going to find out what you are, Oscar Grimstone."

CHAPTER 5

Sally hurried Oscar through the streets. She knew loads of cunning shortcuts, plotting a course through the winding maze of ghost buildings crammed between the office blocks and banks of the city of London.

"How do you remember where to go?" Oscar asked, getting a headache from all the twists and turns.

Sally grinned back at him. "If you've lived in a city for more than a hundred years, you learn your way around, right?" She led him through a muddy medieval square full of smoky stone forges, broken up with a few crooked wooden shop fronts.

She glanced at a pocket watch. "Oops. Better get a move on!"

Around them, Oscar realized the square was sort of . . . stretching. And narrowing. The buildings on either side squeezed inward, and the end began to curve away ahead of them. Sally broke into a run, and Oscar didn't need asking twice. Together, they raced down the stretching, bending street, and out the other side, into a wide Georgian-era avenue.

"What just happened?" Oscar panted.

"Hmmm?" Sally was casually dusting herself down. She glanced back at the moving street, sliding off down the road. "Oh, that. Well, streets in this city have been built over and replaced a lot through history. They have to take it in turns. Smith's Courtyard was destroyed in the Peasant's Revolt and became Crescent Street. Takes you all the way to Victoria. But we don't want to go there, obviously." Oscar blinked. She patted him on the back.

Next, they walked through the swivel doors of a towering glass skyscraper, except Oscar found himself in the walled garden of a Tudor estate. Around him, Oscar could still faintly make out the skyscraper's interior, dark against the shimmering ghost world. A few silhouettes of the living flitted by. As he walked through the figures, he picked up a few thoughts—incredibly boring ones, mostly about "stocks" and "business targets."

Oscar was trying not to lose his head entirely.

They exited the walled garden onto Oxford Street, and soon wound up in St. James's Park. The trees hunched dark and gloomy in the early morning light.

"What are we doing in a park?"

Sally grinned and pointed. "Going there. That's where

I work. We might be able to track down your dad there. I need to draw up a new investigation."

Right in the middle of the park's lake, a ghost tower rose out of the water. It was straight from a horror movie, covered in gargoyles and sinister robed statues. Green gas lamps flickered on either side of an enormous sign that read *Ghost Law Enforcement*.

Lots of ghost policemen were bustling about. Most were arriving on floating carriages pulled by skeletal horses like the one Sir Cedric had driven. Others were in hovercrafts or on motorbikes—one policeman was even riding a giant woolly elephant.

Oscar had to ask. "Is that a mammoth?"

"Bernard? He works with Riot Squad. I heard that there was a bit of trouble earlier at a jousting match."

"Right." Oscar scanned the rest of the vehicles. "Where does it all come from?"

Sally rolled her eyes and gave a sigh. "Well, I think Bernard had some unfinished business with some cavemen who ate him, so he stuck around to get them back when they became ghosts. I hear he was recruited personally by Mr. Mortis. He was a lot more hands-on back then, because there were fewer deaths to deal with. The other police gear is supplied by the Department of Contraptions. Their mechanics begin to think outside the box after working for a few hundred years."

A few police ghosts were escorting ghosts in handcuffs into the building. Sally frowned at the crowd.

"Main door's busy," she said. "Let's try somewhere a bit quieter. I wonder what's going on?" She headed off toward a side entrance.

"Why'd that ghost call you a ghoul back there?" Oscar asked as they casually strolled across the lake. Their feet didn't leave ripples in the water.

"You ask a lot of questions, don't you?" said Sally. "It's a nickname. For police officers, but it kind of became official."

"Ah, right, that makes sense."

"Yeah, best be glad I'm not a real ghoul." Sally's grin slipped. "Actual ghouls like to capture ghosts and feed on their phantasma—kinda like ghost vampires. If you get drained too much, you become constantly hungry. They mostly live on the outskirts, in the cave district. Not a nice area. I wouldn't go there."

Oscar gulped.

"Evening, Bert," said Sally as they pushed through a side door into a room full of heavy old-fashioned furniture.

A fat, balding ghost was lounging with his feet up on a desk. He snorted and nearly fell out of his chair.

"Evenin', Sally," he said. "You caught me napping again. Who's this?"

Sally shrugged. "Oh, just an old friend of mine." She

gave Oscar a little nudge to make sure he didn't say anything. Oscar wondered why she was lying.

"That's fine," Bert said. "But he'd better empty his pockets in the tray. Rules are rules."

"What? Don't embarrass me, Bert. Can't you let him off? We're just popping in for a moment."

Bert shook his head. "HQ's on lockdown. There's orders, down from the tippety-top. Some kind of situation going on. Just pop your things in that tray there, lad. Won't take a moment."

Oscar began to empty his pockets—a few coins, his wallet, his phone, and a little book of sudoku. But the moment the coins left his fingers, all of them turned real and fell right through the ghost tray that Bert was holding.

The coins fell right through the floor as well. There was a soft splash. Oscar managed to grab on to the rest of his stuff just in time to stop it disappearing as well.

Bert's smile vanished. He glared at Sally.

"That coin turned real!" He sounded genuinely shocked. "What game you trying to pull? What's this?"

"It's . . . it's nothing," said Sally. "Heh! Just an accident."

"That's no accident. That's *odd*." Bert ran over to the wall and pressed a big red button. An alarm started ringing, painfully loud.

"You're in a heap of trouble, Sally Cromarty. You shouldn't have tried to pull a fast one on Bert Higgins."

A whole squad of police ghosts burst into the room on the double. They grabbed Oscar and Sally and marched them off to a small, windowless room. The police ghosts locked the heavy door behind them.

"I'm sorry," Oscar said, sitting down at the small table.

"No. I'm sorry," Sally said. "Should have known better than to bring you here."

There were lots of comings and goings outside, and frantic, whispered conversations, but no one came into the room for a long time.

Sally borrowed Oscar's book of sudoku. She paged through it, frowning.

"What is this exactly?" she said eventually. "Are you meant to do this for fun?"

"It's like . . . codes," Oscar said. He'd sniffed a whiff of mockery in her voice. "See . . . I like puzzles."

"That's good," Sally said, "because you are one."

Still no one came. To pass the time, Oscar started to read the faded notices pinned to the board on the wall: various messages about recycling, a note about a collection for Sergeant Fred Bogrum's leaving present before he departed for the Other Side, and a sign-up sheet for the Ghoul cricket team.

Before Oscar could put his name down, the door slammed open. A tall ghost in a long black evening gown strode into the room. She was gripping a cigarette in a long holster between her teeth. Dramatic swirls of hair were piled high on her head.

Sally instantly leapt her to her feet and saluted.

Oscar was too shocked to move. The newcomer would have been a beautiful woman—if half her skin wasn't missing. Beneath chunks of flesh and strings of muscle, white bone gleamed as if it had been oiled.

"So, Mr. Grimstone!" She looked Oscar up and down. Only a few yellowing scraps of tendon held one of her beady eyes in place. Oscar felt like shriveling up into a ball. "What are we to do with you?"

"I—" Oscar began.

"Don't speak unless I tell you to, Grimstone! My name is Lady Margaret Banks. I am the head of the GLE—and you have caused me an enormous amount of trouble—as have you, *young lady.*"

Lady Margaret glared ferociously at Sally. Smoke leaked from her skull as she took a deep drag on her cigarette. Sally didn't flinch.

"I've already interrogated your partner, Sir Cedric. I know what happened. I know what you did. Thank Mortis he had the sense to report it. We've dispatched two teams of memory wipers to Fleet Street and Victoria Embankment. We've narrowly avoided three major breaches. Lucky for you."

She spoke in quick snapped sentences between ferocious

drags on her cigarette. The smoke filled the room and caught in the back of Oscar's throat—a sweet, deathly stink, like rotting flowers and cloves.

"Get your phone," she instructed Oscar. "Then drop it."

Lady Margaret watched with narrowed eyes as Oscar did what he was told. As usual the phone turned real the moment it left his fingers. Oscar made sure to catch it again so it didn't fall through the building to the lake below.

"Do that again."

They all watched as the phone turned solid and then ghostly again as soon as Oscar caught it.

"This breaks all the rules!" Lady Margaret snapped. Somehow she seemed even angrier now. "People and their possessions should not be able to switch between being living and ghost. And paragraph 19,233 of Ghost Immigration Control states that being dead without holding a living world visa or being accompanied by a spirit guide is against the law of the Ministry of Ghosts!"

"I have a theory, ma'am," Sally said. "See, I don't think it's Oscar's fault."

Lady Margaret narrowed her eyes. "A theory?" she snarled, as if theories were things she scraped off her shoe.

Oscar was delighted that Sally had dragged Lady Margaret's terrifying glare away from him, if only for a moment. He was even more delighted that she seemed to be on his side.

In a brisk, official manner, Sally gave Lady Margaret a quick account of what had happened to Oscar in the mortuary.

"We all know that poltergeisting that strong needs a huge amount of phantasma," Sally concluded. "Exposure to the phantasma probably triggered something inside Oscar. That's why his abilities came alive."

"Grimstone!" Lady Margaret snapped back to Oscar. "Describe this man you say you saw outside your house again."

Oscar tried hard to remember. "He had a hat—like an old-fashioned detective—and he was wearing a scarf over his face. I couldn't see much!"

"How convenient!" Lady Margaret didn't look convinced. "That's hardly a description. You remember anything else about this alleged assassin?"

"No," Oscar said, looking down.

"Pff. I don't believe this story!" Lady Margaret said. "Poltergeisting is a Forbidden Craft. I can't think of a single ghost with the power or the knowledge to pull off what you describe. It sounds ridiculous! And I can't believe that you've fallen for this live human's nonsense, Detective Cromarty."

"With respect, Lady Margaret," Sally said, "there were very high levels of residual phantasma in the funeral house. Something happened there."

"Why would any ghost want anything to do with this idiot?" Lady Margaret asked. She seemed determined to ignore what Sally was saying. "Ridiculous!"

"I think I can prove it, ma'am," Sally replied.

"Go on, then," Lady Margaret snapped.

"So . . ." Sally gave Oscar an encouraging smile before she continued. "Can you think of anyone who's dead who might have a bone to pick with you or your mother?"

Oscar thought for a bit.

"No," he said. "We're always very nice to the dead."

"And how long has your family been in the funeral business?" Sally asked.

Lady Margaret leaned in like a cobra ready to strike.

"Since my grandma—my dad's mother started it." Oscar was so unnerved by Lady Margaret's glaring eyes that he started to babble. "Her name was Barbara—and she was a single mum, very unusual in those days for a woman to run a successful business. No one knew who my grandfather was. . . ."

Lady Margaret snorted with disgust.

"I fail to see how this *heartwarming* story is in any way relevant, Detective. You've proved nothing. There's been some kind of accident. That's what's happened."

Before Sally could argue again, the door opened, and a short, plump man rushed into the room. His tweed suit was a disheveled mess. At least six pocket watches dangled on long golden chains across his chest. He was examining one of them as he came into the room.

"So late, so inconvenient," he muttered, throwing his briefcase onto the table.

Lady Margaret's demeanor transformed in an instant. Half-panicked, she stood ramrod-straight, exchanged her frown for an ingratiating grin, and quickly crushed her cigarette out on the ground with a snap of her stilettoed heel.

"Sir." She bowed deeply as she shook the newcomer's hand. She had to bow deeply because she was about three feet taller than him. "This is truly an honor, only you needn't have come. This is just a small matter, practically resolved already. . . ."

The two of them started whispering, too low for Oscar to hear.

The man glanced at Sally. She was standing to attention too and caught his eye.

"Sir Merriweather Northcote," she whispered out of the corner of her mouth. "Second in charge of the Ministry. Mortis's right-hand man. Big, big, big cheese. *Very* important."

Turning from Lady Margaret, Northcote rummaged through his briefcase until he pulled out a sheet of paper. He frowned at it, then looked straight at Oscar. His weak, watery eyes gave nothing away.

"So you can turn into a ghost, eh?" he said.

"Um . . ." Oscar wasn't sure if that was true.

"Quick, boy! Do you know how valuable my time is?"

"No?" Oscar answered truthfully.

"Is he an idiot?" Northcote snapped. "Does he know how much Mortis's damned paperwork is towering up on my desk, solely because of his antics this night?"

"He is both unnaturally stupid," Lady Margaret said, "and unnatural."

"Not a winning combination," said Northcote. "Now . . ." He fumbled around in his various pockets. "Where are my blasted glasses?!"

"On your head, sir," Sally said with a straight face.

Northcote glared at her. "You aren't much better, Detective. This boy is extremely dangerous, and you've let him run riot. It will be noted on your permanent record. Lucky for you that you've proved reliable in the past."

"Very poor judgment." Lady Margaret glared daggers at Sally. "Not what the GLE expects in our senior officers. The boy is certainly dangerous. The detective should have sensed that immediately."

Oscar was about to say that was ridiculous. *Dangerous!* How could he be dangerous? And then he thought about the wilting flowers—and how everything he touched died—and his own protest died in his throat. He looked down at his knees, blinking. What if they were right? Maybe he *was* dangerous. *Maybe* that's why his dad had died. . . .

"It's not his fault, sir!" Sally yelled.

The fact that she was standing up for him made Oscar feel even worse. He hadn't told Sally the whole truth, had he? He hadn't mentioned his Curse.

"Fault is not the issue," snapped Northcote. "Keeping a lid on this little problem is. Lady Margaret, I trust you will personally *contain* this now. Send the boy home, until we can work out what to do with him. This is a delicate time, as you know—any hint of an upset could be very significant."

"Of course, sir!" Lady Margaret bowed. "Not a whisper will leak out. You can count on the GLE to do its duty, my personal guarantee."

"Good." Northcote pulled three watches out of his waistcoat, inspected them all with a sigh. "So much to do, so little time. But that's the curse of being late, eh!"

He bustled out of the room.

Lady Margaret's oily simper vanished, and a stormy scowl took its place. The sudden change of expression on her shredded face was horrific. Oscar had never realized that so many muscles went into a frown.

"Take this problem home, Detective. Make sure it disappears. Boy—you will not change into a ghost again. When the Ministry knows its position, you will be contacted. Have I made myself clear?"

"But what about the ghost that attacked him?" Sally

said. "The man in the hat! That might be even more dangerous."

Oscar was impressed that Sally still dared to argue with Lady Margaret.

"I am not interested in your theories, *girl*. I am interested in doing what my superiors tell me to do. You would do well to follow my example." The threat was clear.

With one last scowl for good luck, Lady Margaret left the room.

CHAPTER

6

Sally took Oscar to the untidy office she shared with Sir Cedric. The headquarters of the GLE was a chaos of corridors and staircases, full of busy ghosts bustling around. There were huge crystal chandeliers hanging from the ornate ceilings. The cornices were decorated with more gargoyles, whose monstrous faces overlooked tapestries: some of the images depicted famous arrests, and others were portraits of ex–police chiefs. Sally's office was high up, near the top of the tower. The door was carved in spiky gothic letters with her and Cedric's initials and the words *Detectives, Phantasmic Breaches, and Forbidden Crafts.*

Inside, the room was bathed in moonlight from a magnificent arched window that gave a view over the park and the city beyond: the sprawling jumble of living and dead cities, falling all over each other—half-sparkling, half-dark.

Around the stone-flagged office, documents and forms and folders were piled into teetering mountain ranges on every available surface. Comic books and old-fashioned serial storybooks poked out of the stacks. Oscar also noticed a giant jar of candy. Sir Cedric wasn't there.

"That hag called me girl!" Sally was still fuming about Lady Margaret. "She doesn't care about cases or helping the dead. All she cares about is sucking up to the chief and getting promoted. You know Lady Margaret's only been dead for fifteen years!"

"Don't worry . . . I'm sure you'll get there one day," Oscar said.

"If I wanted to get *there*, I would have done it last century," Sally snapped. "Who'd want to be Lady Margaret? All she does is toady up to Mr. Mortis and push paper around. She's an idiot!"

"Why does she look so . . ."

"Rat-bitten? Because she thinks it's more dramatic, I suppose. We ghosts can appear pretty much how we like. Though most of us prefer to look like we used to. It just feels right, you know."

Oscar had always wanted to have long hair, but his mum had never let him. He thought hard about his hair growing for a second, then put his hand to his neck to find . . .

"Gosh," Oscar said.

"Yeah," said Sally, cocking her head to one side. "I think that suits you better. Do you want a Gobstopper?"

"Um . . . yes, please." Oscar took one of the round hard candies and popped it in his mouth. It tasted almost right—a sort of dusty lemonish flavor. His new hair felt a bit heavy when he moved his head.

Sally had pulled out a typewriter and began typing furiously. After a minute, she ripped the sheet of paper from the machine and held it up in the air.

It vanished.

"Good. Off to the visa people at Ghost Immigration. That'll start the ball rolling on finding your dad. If he ever stuck around in the Living World and got a visa, they'll know," she said.

Oscar pointed at the typewriter. "How did that . . ." He trailed off, realizing he was asking another question, which Sally didn't like him doing.

"Phantasma," replied Sally. "It's not just people who have it. It's everywhere, and it can be harnessed like an energy source. That message was just powered through the phantasmic barrier, across the void, straight to those pen-pushing bureaucrats. Voilà! So what about you? I'm supposed to take you home now."

"I don't want to go home," said Oscar quickly. "I want to find out what's going on. . . . And thank you for looking for my dad."

"No problem." Sally looked at him. It was another one

of her long, penetrating stares. It felt like her gray eyes were scalpels, peeling him apart. It was doubly odd coming from a thirteen-year-old girl.

"Tell me, Oscar," she said eventually, "why do you want to stay a ghost? Normally that's the last thing a living person wants to be."

Oscar had to stop and think. It was pretty bonkers when you put it like that. He wondered again if he should tell her the truth.

You see the thing is, Sally, I'm a freak. I kill things I touch.

He couldn't bring himself to say it.

"Well . . . someone tried to kill me. I can't just wait for them to attack me again."

"Sure," Sally said. "That makes sense, but do you really want to stay dead?"

"Yes," Oscar said, surprised by how sure he felt. "I like it here. It's like . . . here I make more sense, you know? And I can run really fast and I don't have to use my crutch. . . . This is basically the most exciting thing that's ever happened to me!"

Sally grinned. "That's good. Because I would have taken you back if you wanted. But we're not going to do that now."

"What are we going to do?"

"Really annoy Lady Margaret."

Sally scribbled a note to Cedric, explaining that he had

to cover for her for a bit. Then they borrowed a carriage and horses and rattled north as if a full-on riot of blood-crazed knights was behind them. A hour later, they turned onto a small nondescript street. It was dark, and everyone was still asleep.

"Here we are," Sally said, pulling at the reins. "I'm the red door."

Her house was modest, practically indistinguishable from a thousand other London terraced houses—except that it was slipped inside another, real house—like a hand inside a glove.

The front door wasn't locked either. Inside, he found a bigger mess than in her office. Mounds of papers. Half-read books in teetering towers. Three jam sandwiches forgotten on the sofa—and bags of sweets everywhere. They were all made by the same sweetmaker: Mr. Werther. Gas lamps gave light from where they hung on the walls, lending strange shapes to the garish Victorian textured wallpaper.

The living room was aglow in a constant shimmering fire that burned in the grate. A large bulletin board was covered in notes and strings. It looked like a spider had started a scrapbook.

Oscar tiptoed through the clutter to investigate. In the center of the board, at the heart of the maze of string, was a stiff old black-and-white photograph of a Victorian man and woman. The woman was pretty, and her familiarly high cheekbones and sharp sparkling eyes looked so much like Sally's that Oscar knew she must be her mother. The man was in a detective uniform. Next to them, a tattered Wanted poster caught Oscar's eye.

Hieronymus Jones

The diabolical alchemist and inventor is wanted
in connection with forty-two outstanding crimes,
including ghost murder, mischievous and malignant
hauntings, inappropriate use of phantasma with
intent to harm, and the possession of forbidden
devices and contraptions in contravention of Article
15, 23, and 234 of the Ghost Convention of 1934.
Jones died in 1888 but is unlikely to dress in Victorian
clothes. He is a master of disguise and has been
known to hide in plain sight. Do not approach
unless suitably shielded. Please alert the authorities
immediately if you have any information about this
highly dangerous ghost.

Sally came into the room.

"Did you catch him yet?" Oscar asked, pointing at the poster.

Sally's eyes blazed. Oscar was surprised at how furious she looked.

"No," she said. "That's not important. Just a cold case I'm working on." With a grunt of effort, she grabbed the board and flipped it over.

"Sorry," Oscar said. "I didn't—"

"It's time to start a new case," Sally interrupted. "The mystery of Oscar Grimstone."

They both got to work. Sally wrote *SUSPECT*. Beneath she gave a profile of the attacker: *Wears hat and scarf. Trained in poltergeisting.* Oscar helped her pin a piece of string to another bundle of information labeled *WITNESS*. There was a profile of Oscar: *Oscar Grimstone, twelve years and seven months old, from Little Worthington. Able to turn into a ghost. Phantasma readings off the charts.*

Once again, Oscar wondered if he should tell Sally about his Curse. That he killed things he touched. He glanced at her. She was scribbling on a note card, eyes gleaming, filled with purpose. Maybe he could trust her?

But before Oscar could decide, a piece of paper suddenly appeared in the air. Sally snatched it up and read it quickly, then handed it Oscar.

NO SIGN JULIAN GRIMSTONE

"Does that mean he's not here?" said Oscar. His voice wobbled. He hadn't realized how much hope had built up inside him. Tears formed in his eyes.

"No—it just means that there's no record of him in ghost London right now." Sally put a hand on Oscar's shoulder. "But don't worry, Oscar. Plenty of ghosts slip through the cracks. Just means we need to do more digging."

Oscar took a deep breath. "Okay. Can we do that now?"

Sally stuck a card on the bulletin board, beneath the profile of Oscar: *Julian Grimstone*. "Sure. If we find out about your dad, we might discover what you are exactly. Maybe he'll have the answers."

Sally turned from the room.

"So where do we go?" Oscar said, following her out the front door.

"The place is kind of hard to describe."

They climbed into Sally's cart and galloped through the streets of London. This time, Sally pushed the skeleton horses so recklessly through the oncoming traffic, that Oscar closed his eyes the whole way. It was really hard to remember that the bus you were riding toward was not going to smash you and your ghost carriage into a million pieces.

He was very relieved when Sally drew up the horses outside the British Library.

The normal, living person's building was shut up for the night, but a small, discreet wooden door shimmered a ghostly silver in the redbrick wall. A flickering green lantern above the door illuminated a sign that read *Department of Records*.

"This is where they keep track of everyone who has ever lived and died," Sally explained. "And everyone on the Other Side as well. We can find your dad's file, and yours too. But I warn you: Try to stay calm, all right? You'll get used to it after a few breaths."

"Stay calm? What do you mea— ARGH!"

Oscar saw what was on the other side of the door, and his mind seemed to explode.

It was the largest set of shelves he had ever seen. They went up and down and sideways *forever*, thousands upon thousands of shelves stretching as far as the eye could see, all neatly filled with little manila folders and scrolls. The distances were so vast and so impossible that his brain couldn't take it all in and it felt like it was constricting in his skull. He wanted to tear his hair out and scream. He shut his eyes again to try to cope.

"Just breathe," murmured Sally. "And don't look down."

But Oscar couldn't help but look down. "Aaagh!" he shouted, clutching Sally's sleeve.

They were standing on a small platform made out of a kind of thin wire mesh. Through the holes in this mesh,

Oscar saw a very long drop. There was no bottom, only a dim, pulsing blackness.

The platform clung to the side of this giant shelf cliff like a bureaucratic bird's nest. The platform was about ten feet square. It had room for a desk with a small brass bell on it. Behind the desk sat a very neatly dressed ghost, with a trim beard and a turban.

"Try to concentrate on my face, young ghost," he said kindly. "Newcomers have told me they find that reassuring. I am the Archivist."

The Archivist was the oldest-looking person Oscar had ever seen. But he had warm eyes and that helped.

"I'm just showing my new colleague the ropes," Sally said. "This place gets newbies every time, doesn't it?"

"It does. Were you just here to scare him?" the Archivist asked. "Or did you have a request in mind?"

"We do. We're after two files: Oscar Grimstone—birthday January 26, 2006, and his father, Julian. . . ."

"Hold tight, please," the Archivist said.

"Argh!" Oscar shouted for a third time, as the small platform plunged down the giant cliff shelf, zigzagging like a drop of water running down a windowpane.

After they'd fallen for what felt like *three miles,* they came to a sudden stop in front of a shelf that looked exactly like all the others. Without hesitating, the Archivist walked from his desk, turned, and plucked a small brown folder from a row of a hundred that looked just like it.

The Archivist clicked his fingers. A huge leather-bound ledger appeared from thin air with a rustle of paper. "Please sign here before you look at the files," he said.

Oscar couldn't sign his own name without giving himself away, so he called himself Gary Stevens—the bully who lived on their street. There was only one other name in the ledger. Three weeks ago, someone called Jessie Mur had signed out Oscar's file. After Sally signed her name neatly, she tapped the stranger's name with the quill, catching Oscar's eye.

She glanced at the Archivist. "Funny name. D'you remember what they looked like?"

The Archivist chuckled. "I remember everyone who visits me. Jessie Mur wore a wide-brimmed hat and a scarf wrapped around his face."

Oscar just managed to stop himself letting out a gasp.

"I don't know why everyone's so interested in this file," the Archivist said, checking that they'd signed. "A very ordinary boy, this Oscar Grimstone."

"That's why we're using him for training purposes," said Sally. "We've identified him as the most boring boy in Britain. He's a marvel of the ordinary, really."

Oscar was about to protest but remembered he was

supposed to be Gary Stevens, not Oscar Grimstone, and the words choked in his throat. The Archivist gave another dry chuckle. "How funny." He went back to his desk and began looking through a list of parchment.

Oscar and Sally eagerly paged through the bundle of forms and reports. The papers were in chronological order, with the most recent papers at the front, and documented every important event in Oscar's life so far. They were very up to date. Already, the strange events of this evening were in the file—there were several eyewitness reports of Oscar's antics near the bone ship, as well as Sir Cedric's notes about investigating Oscar's house.

As they read through Oscar's middle school years, Sally got annoyed.

"This Gary Stevens sure likes to pick on you," she muttered. "Why'd he call you all these names? And flush your head down the toilet? And why'd you call yourself after him in the book?"

Oscar shrugged. It was funny—Gary Stevens seemed like the least of his problems now. Because he hadn't told Sally the full truth, he was glad that the file didn't seem to mention anything about the Curse. Very little else was missed. Oscar's fourth-grade clarinet exam results were noted, as were his granny's death and an award he'd received from a local library when he was seven. It was very weird to see your life laid out like this.

Though, as they grew close to the day of his father's death, Oscar grew very nervous. He hadn't thought of this before, but what if he found out that he'd killed his father? What if the book showed it was all his fault? This was Oscar's worst fear. His hand trembled as he held the book.

"Don't worry, mate," Sally said. "You really love your dad, don't you?"

Oscar nodded.

"We all do," Sally said. "Just remember that it doesn't stop with death either. Love lasts, see?"

This made sense to Oscar. "You know how I become a ghost?" he asked.

"I'd wondered."

"I just think about my dad—that's all it takes."

"Exactly—sometimes the bonds of love are so strong, they keep a connection beyond death. Maybe your dad's love provides you with the link you need between the worlds."

Oscar smiled at the thought and turned the page.

He froze. He could barely look at the page. It was very plain—just an excerpt from the police report, saying that his dad had died in a car crash. The fear of what really happened that night had been haunting Oscar since he'd first begun to find out about his Curse. He scanned through hurriedly.

Nothing about a Curse. Nothing about Oscar killing him.

Oscar felt relieved—and then a stab of white-hot guilt at the relief. What kind of monster was relieved that their father was killed in a car crash?

Sally carried on flicking through the file.

"You were a charming baby," she muttered. "You won a prize! Look—hang on—what's this?!"

At the back of the folder was a page that recorded Oscar's birth. It looked like this:

Oscar Grimstone born January 26, 2006.

Then there was a *deathday*.

Oscar Grimstone died ~~July 14, 2007~~ MM

The deathday was crossed out with a neat pen stroke and signed in an elegant hand *MM*.

"Holy Jack O'Lantern!" said Sally.

"But . . . how can that be?" Oscar asked. "That's . . . the day of the car accident."

He felt the world spinning around him. The fear clutched tight again. Was he supposed to be dead? Was that why he was cursed? Why he was able to turn into a ghost?

It took all his concentration to keep from turning bodily with the shock.

"And here's me calling you the most boring boy in

Britain," said Sally. "Looks like someone helped you cheat death. Lucky for you . . . I suppose." Something in her voice made Oscar glance at her face.

She looked young all of a sudden, scared.

"Who's MM?" he asked, looking at the initials next to his deathday. "That's who crossed it out, isn't it?"

"MM? He's only the biggest cheese of them all: the first Minister of the Ministry of Ghosts, Mr. Mortis himself! Your lot call him Death, or the Grim Reaper. Of course, people who've met him say he isn't so grim—apparently he likes to collect mugs."

"Are you serious?" Oscar said, heart thumping. "*Death himself* stopped me from dying?" He tried to picture a skeleton with a scythe, signing his life back into existence. "Why?"

"Only Mortis knows." Sally grinned grimly. "Hey! Chin up, Oscar! We're getting to the bottom of why you're so peculiar. I wonder what kind of mistake was made?"

"Mistake?" Oscar couldn't keep the hysteria out of his voice.

"Someone must have made a mistake for Mr. Mortis to intervene. He's usually way too busy to take an interest in small matters like this. Very odd indeed. And this is odd too—look, do you see how this sheet's been sliced in half?"

She was right. The bottom half of the death sheet had been snipped away.

"I wonder who took it. I'd wager it was the ghost in the hat, eh? Jessie Mur."

Oscar nodded, struggling to put it all together. The stranger who tried to kill him. The Curse. The dad he couldn't remember. The dad who'd died on the day that he was meant to. And it made it even worse to know that Mr. Mortis had saved Oscar's life but not spared his father's.

"I suppose that must be why you've got ghost powers, Oscar," Sally said. Her voice came from very far away. "Because you've already died . . ."

Yes, Oscar wanted to add. *And that's why I kill living things when I touch them too. I should have died and now I'm cursed.*

"What you thinking about, Oscar?" asked Sally. "It's a lot to take in. Are you all right?"

Oscar didn't tell her. What would she think of his Curse? What if she stopped helping him, or handed him in to Lady Margaret, who might send him aboard that bone ship in case he hurt anyone, or broke the rules too much. He could feel the lie getting bigger and bigger, like an anchor dragging him down.

He blinked.

"Can we see Julian Grimstone's file now?" He looked over at the Archivist.

"Of course, young ghost," the Archivist said. All of a sudden the platform zoomed upward, moving so fast that the shelves blurred. Oscar felt as if he was dragging his stomach eighteen stories behind him.

Once the platform screeched to a stop, the Archivist pulled another file from a shelf and handed it over.

"Julian Grimstone," the Archivist said. "As requested." He resumed his work, dipping his quill in a pot of ink and scrawling on a long scroll.

Oscar opened it with trembling hands. The first thing he saw was a piece of paper with a big red stamp saying *OTHER SIDE*.

"Oh," said Sally, staring at it. "Oh dear."

"What's that?" Oscar asked.

"The Other Side?" Sally said. "Well, that's the place where your soul goes to rest. Only it's not really resting— you get the eternity that you deserve. A Life Maker in the Department of Afterlives takes a look at what you did during your life, and what you liked best, and then you get to do that forever. It's not a bad deal, really. Only department that Mr. Mortis gets personally involved in."

She was babbling. There was something she didn't want to say.

"So can I go see him over there?" Oscar asked sharply. "I could go on that bone ship, couldn't I?"

Sally looked him in the eye. "No, Oscar," she said gently. "Not unless you want to stay dead. It's a one-way ticket to the Other Side, I'm afraid."

Somehow, this was much worse than finding out you were already dead and probably cursed. "I see," he said in a small voice. "But it's nice over there?"

"Take a look," Sally said. "It'll be here at the back."

Sally flicked through his father's file; Oscar, watching desperately, wished he could read it all.

"There," Sally said. "He's doing well."

Looking at how Julian Grimstone spent his days, his personal afterlife sounded pretty perfect to Oscar. The Life Maker must have done a good job.

During the day, he built furniture and carved sculptures out of driftwood. He went to punk gigs in the evening. Once or twice a week, he went for a long walk along the coast or took a bike into town. Every morning was Sunday, and all the papers were delivered to his house along with a full English breakfast with extra sausages and black pudding. The newspapers always had a section about how his family was doing, Oscar in particular.

"See," Sally said. "He's keeping an eye on you."

"Can I talk to him?"

"No. I'm sorry, Oscar," Sally said. "Like I told you, it's a one-way thing to the Other Side. But he'll be watching you, following everything you do."

"Right," Oscar said.

"It could be a lot worse, trust me," Sally said quietly. "Not everyone gets such a peaceful death."

Oscar nodded. He couldn't speak just then. Hot tears were running down his face—and a great bursting sob was building up inside him.

"I love you, Dad," he whispered.

He hoped his dad could hear him.

CHAPTER

7

"Hey! Look at that!" Sally said from over Oscar's shoulder, jabbing at the very last page. The edge in Sally's voice made Oscar jump and grab the railing of the platform that hovered over the endless abyss of files.

"Here's our Jessie Mur, at it again," she said.

The page that recorded Oscar's dad's birth and death was sliced in half, just like Oscar's had been.

Oscar's cheeks burned. He felt a deep fury far stronger than when seeing his own file sabotaged, or finding out the name of the person who had tried to kill him.

Now this Jessie Mur had messed with his dad, and he was going to pay.

"We've got to get him!" Oscar said. "Or her. Can we take these folders with us?"

"We'd need approval from the Ministry," Sally said, "and that can take some time."

"A few days, right? We can wait that long."

Sally chuckled. "Try a few decades—if we're *lucky*. Ghost business moves slow. Of course, things are faster if the bigwigs are on your side—but we're not exactly Lady Margaret's cup of tea right now, are we?"

"All right, then we steal them," Oscar said. "Simple." He felt surprised at his own daring.

Sally looked a little worried. "I'm all for bending the rules when it gets the job done, but you have to be careful when messing with the rules round here. That Archivist is a powerful being—he's more than a regular ghost. How else can you keep the names of a hundred billion dead souls in your head? Apparently he was around with Mortis in the beginning. What I'm saying is, that old Archivist loves his files more than anything—and if he catches us, he might trap us in here forever, or turn us into a shelf or a potted plant, or worse."

"We have to, Sally. I can't wait a few decades."

Sally tapped her chin. "I hear you. But, still, it's a big risk."

Oscar had a sudden thought about how he could convince her. He sighed. "I guess you're right. Lady Margaret wouldn't want us doing it, and we should probably obey her orders."

Sally's brow crinkled. "Hold on! We can't let that old bag tell us what to do! Right, we're doing this! But we need a very good plan."

Oscar thought fast. "How about if I pretend I'm feeling ill . . . so I need to leave . . . and then you try to distract the old coot, ask for some more papers, keep him occupied."

"Right—and then you make a run for it while I'm talking . . ." Sally's brow furrowed. "You know, that's not bad at all! Might just work. You ready?"

"Yes." Oscar patted the folders inside his jacket. "You go first."

Sally moved over to the desk and began asking for a long list of folders. With every request, the platform swooped up and down across the shelves. Oscar didn't have to pretend too hard that he was feeling nauseated. It was like traveling on the world's most intense roller coaster.

"I think I'm going to be ill," he moaned.

"Careful, young ghost," the Archivist said. "Not on my files! For Mortis's sake!"

"Oh no!" Oscar gasped. "I can feel it coming up! Urkch!" He dry-heaved and clapped a hand over his mouth, as if he could barely hold his stomach down.

"For Hecate's sake, hold it in!" The Archivist turned pale, and the platform sped across the shelves faster than ever. It came crashing to a halt in front of the door that they'd first come in.

"Out! Out! Through there!" the Archivist cried, pointing to the door.

Oscar stumbled outside, doubled over as if locked in mortal combat with his stomach. He found himself back on Euston Road with cars and buses streaking past. A faint light in the east showed that dawn was coming.

About ten minutes later, Sally emerged as well. She was grinning broadly.

"Good job!" She clapped Oscar on the back. "You really sold that—and once we'd chatted for a while and talked about turban care, he forgot all about you. I think he's lonely."

"We really did it!" Oscar said.

"You did! That was a great plan." Sally gave a long, low whistle. A moment later, their horse and carriage trotted up obediently to meet them.

"Oh, I asked him a few questions too." She climbed up and took the reins. "Tried to look at Jessie Mur's file. Doesn't exist. It's a made-up name."

"Of course it is!" Oscar said, surprised once again at how angry he felt. "But he could have used that alias before."

"Let's hope so, eh?" Sally reached under her seat and pulled out her typewriter again. Her fingers clattered quickly across the keys.

"I'll send a message to Sir Cedric asking him to run the name," she explained. "Won't take a minute."

Oscar watched as she ripped the sheet of paper from the machine and held it up in the air. After a few seconds, it disappeared.

"That goes straight to his desk?" Oscar asked.

"Exactly! Right on top of a big pile of papers I imagine. Bet you living folk wish you had such an easy way to send messages back in your world, eh?"

For a second, Oscar debated explaining the internet to Sally—but then decided it would be a waste of time.

"Instant messages!" he said. "Wow! You ghosts *really* have it all."

Sally gave him a funny look.

"Hey, I've got an idea," Oscar said. "Can you send one of your amazing messages to Mr. Mortis? We could ask him why he saved me."

"No, it'll definitely be blocked."

"Then let's go see him. Surely he's the best person to clear this up."

"He's not really a person—more of . . . a god, I suppose. But I imagine he would. Only problem is very few ghosts get to see him. I don't know anyone who's actually met him—apart from the Archivist and a few other hotshots. And Northcote, of course—he's Mr. Mortis's private secretary."

Oscar remembered the small stressed-out man with all the pocket watches who had come into the room when

Lady Margaret was questioning them. Mr. Mortis sounded almost impossible to get to. But there had to be a way.

"We'll get into his office somehow," Oscar said. After his success at burglary, he felt full of purpose—like they could do anything they wanted, no matter how impossible. Besides, he had his powers. He could turn back and forth from ghost to bone—and that had to be a help.

"My, you're really getting into this, aren't you, Oscar?" Sally shook her head. "Maybe we can't fail? Let's give it a shot!"

With a flick of the reins, the carriage shot off down the road. Oscar was feeling so determined he didn't even flinch when they drove straight through the oncoming number 73 bus.

The head offices of the Ministry were near Bank Underground Station, right in the heart of the oldest parts of London.

The entrance, which bulged from the side of a tall, modern glass skyscraper like the architect had suddenly gone mad, was an ancient Roman temple with thick columns and creepy, blank-eyed statues glaring down.

Inside, long corridors and winding staircases led Sally and Oscar up through London's history. They passed

Viking shields and silver death masks, faded tapestries with medieval hunting scenes, gilded pillars and highly detailed models of ancient ships, mighty castles and long-forgotten temples. Gradually, as they rose through the building, the decoration got more modern and they began to see more ghosts too: clerks bustling about with more piles of those ever-present manila folders, porters dragging tea urns the size of tugboats, and frown-faced secretaries taking dictation from speaking tubes.

The building was like a maze, but Sally moved through it confidently. So confidently, in fact, that no one challenged their right to be there until they were just outside Mr. Mortis's office.

The most eccentric-looking receptionist that Oscar had ever seen sat at a desk. She had spiky glasses like butterfly wings, purple hair, and a lemon-sour smile.

"What are *you* doing *here*?" she sneered.

"We'd like to see Mr. Mortis," Sally explained. "It's very urgent."

"Do you have an appointment?" the receptionist asked.

"No," Oscar said. "But—"

"No one sees Mr. Mortis without an appointment." The receptionist opened a drawer in her desk and pulled out an enormous leather-bound book. It must have weighed about the same as a small car, but she handled it deftly, slowly turning the thick parchment pages and running her finger down the list of appointments.

She carried on through her tome for a very long time, and none of Sally's coughs or Oscar's nervous foot-tapping had any effect on her speed at all. Oscar could feel Sally's frustration rising with every page.

At last, after about ten minutes of scanning, the receptionist tapped her finger on a line and looked up.

"Ah, yes! You'll be pleased to know I've found a space where we can fit you in." She smiled wide, like a crocodile inviting a small fish into its mouth.

"Great!" Oscar exclaimed. "When? Today?"

"You'll have to wait a little longer than that." The receptionist's smile broadened. "Not too long, though . . . I've an opening on the last Tuesday afternoon in March 2058. . . . The twenty-fifth, I think. Does that work?"

"Forty years! No, it absolutely doesn't!" Sally growled. "You onion-swilling old trout! You prancing old prune! You made us wait all that time for that!" Oscar had to hold her back from going for the receptionist's throat.

The receptionist's smile glittered even more brightly. She had clearly died just for the joy of moments like these. With a discreet nod, she called security.

"Show these two the way out, please," she murmured, slamming her book shut and placing it back in the drawer.

Oscar was about to argue, until he saw the two men who had emerged from the shadows. One of them was a Viking warrior with a necklace of skulls around his neck. The other was a vast sumo wrestler, whose glistening rolls of oiled fat wobbled as he waddled toward them. They were both the largest men, or ghosts, that Oscar had ever seen.

Sally looked like she was ready to fight them too.

"Let's go, Sally," he whispered, tugging her away before she was flattened.

Outside, day was finally breaking on what had unquestionably been the longest night of Oscar's life. The sun was rising just behind the tall church nearby, but Oscar realized he couldn't feel the warmth on his skin. It was an odd feeling.

There are things you miss being dead.

He didn't feel tired either, which was odder still, because he had been running around all night. Even so, the aura of invincibility that he'd been enjoying had definitely slipped. There was clearly no easy way to get to Mr. Mortis. Their investigation had hit an obstacle.

"Forty years!" Sally yelled, still fuming. "It's ghosts like her that make me wish there really was a hell. She'd fit in perfectly. Did you see how much she enjoyed that?"

Oscar didn't answer. The morning sun glinted off the

marble tombstones in the churchyard. Oscar remembered that Mr. Jenkinson's funeral was going to start in three hours. He still hadn't finished dressing his body.

"Sally, I should go home. My mum's going to be really worried if I'm not there when she wakes up."

"No problem." Sally whistled for the carriage. "Won't take a minute. But I'm not letting that old trout beat me. We have to try something else. There must be a way to get Mr. Mortis's attention. We can carry on the investigation later. In the meantime, I will try to come up with some other leads."

Oscar was quiet for most of the trip back home. The night's madness was catching up with him at last.

Sally kept on cursing the receptionist. She got even angrier the more she thought about it.

"That's the problem with being dead. We've got too much time to waste. It's ridiculous. . . ."

Oscar tuned out her complaining. The carriage was moving so quickly that the whole world blurred around them. That was kind of how he felt too: everything was happening so fast that he couldn't come to grips with it. Maybe if he had a sleep—or even better, a cup of tea—his life would start making sense.

Before he knew it, they were rolling up Marigold Street. The solid little houses looked as cheerful and quiet as ever. It was hard to believe that they were real. Now Oscar was in ghost form, the living buildings had become dulled in color, and everything seemed as thin and flimsy as a stage set.

"Righto, here we are." Sally hadn't stopped plotting for a second. "I'll pick you up in the evening. And I've had a thought about what I can do to help the investigation. I'll pay a visit to every ghost milliner in town. That's a hat shop to you. There're only three or four in London, and maybe one will tell me all about the ghost that bought a big floppy hat. You still with us, Oscar?"

Oscar blinked and nodded. "Yeah, sorry. Um, it's all just a little bit overwhelming. Thanks for . . . thanks for everything, Sally."

"Don't mention it." She gave him a wink and watched as he climbed down from the carriage.

As Oscar searched his pocket for his keys, he saw his crutch lying on the ground behind the bush where he'd chucked it away.

That moment felt like years ago.

With a deep sigh, he picked it up. Then, with a rising sense of dread, he turned himself back from ghostly form into his human body. Instantly, the buildings grew more vivid and the sounds of the living world returned: wind through the prim bushes and the blare of televisions.

Oscar felt like the sky had fallen in on him, and his

bones had turned to lead—all at the same time. He took a step forward and stumbled. His bad leg was aching, but that was nothing compared to the tiredness he felt. His bed was very far away. It felt like a colossal effort to get there.

It was at this moment that the person Oscar least wanted to see in the whole world came running toward him—Gary Stevens, out for an early morning jog.

Oscar was too tired to move, and Gary was too much of a bully to care.

"Out of my way, limpy," he muttered as he elbowed past Oscar, shoving him to the pavement. It hurt.

Oscar suddenly realized that he didn't have to take this anymore. He turned ghostly. The tiredness fell away. Gary Stevens gave a gasp of utter terror as Oscar disappeared.

Gary backed away slowly, looking round to try to see where Oscar had gone. "What's happening?" he muttered. "What's this? Some kind of trick?"

"Haunt him, Oscar!" yelled Sally, who'd seen the whole thing.

Oscar crept around behind Gary. He turned bodily just long enough to whisper, "Boo!" then turned into a ghost.

Gary Stevens's head whipped round. He screamed like a frightened child and ran away.

He sprinted right through where Oscar stood in ghost form. Once again, Oscar caught just a sniff of his thoughts as their bodies were together. There was a large dose of terror, a sort of purple wash of complete panic, and something else, very strange.

Oscar was certain that Gary Stevens hadn't recognized him. *Maybe he just didn't notice who I was,* Oscar wondered. *And it is pretty dark.* But Oscar felt uneasy—like something wasn't right.

He and Sally watched the bully sprint away down the road.

"Good work, Oscar!" Sally said. "If an examiner had seen you, they'd give you a pass in your Haunting exams on the spot."

Oscar frowned. Not being recognized by Gary had rather taken the shine off his victory. They'd only seen each other nearly every day for twelve and a half years.

"You look dead tired, Oscar," Sally said.

"Ho, ho," Oscar said.

"Have a kip! We'll get to the bottom of this or my name ain't Sally Cromarty."

"Hope so. See you later, Sally." Oscar turned bodily, and the tiredness came crashing down once again.

He tried to turn the front door key quietly, but the latch squeaked all the same. As he opened the door, he reached for his spare crutch, which he always kept in the umbrella stand by the door. If he was feeling as bad as this, he'd need two crutches to get up the stairs.

Weirdly, the crutch wasn't there. Oscar groaned before dragging himself upstairs, trying to tread softly and keep his heavy breathing as quiet as he could. As he passed his mother's room, he heard her talking on the phone.

Great, he thought. *That means she hasn't heard me.*

He almost collapsed as he slipped into his room and didn't bother switching the light on, instead feeling his way toward his bed in the corner of the room. He had never ever needed his bed as much as he did right now, and couldn't even be bothered to get undressed. He just wanted to lie down and sleep forever. In fact, he was so tired that he didn't notice what was wrong until he tried to pull back his quilt. His hand brushed thin air.

What?

Oscar hobbled back to the light switch and flicked it on.

His bed wasn't there anymore.

He blinked, closed his eyes, counted to ten, and looked again.

It wasn't just his bed. Everything was gone.

There was a bed, but it was in the other corner of the room. And it wasn't Oscar's bed. It was someone else's— someone super lame. The cheerful skeleton-decorated bedcover he'd had since he was ten had been replaced by an ugly flowery comforter and starched white sheets. All his horror film posters were gone too—even his *Ghostbusters II* original—and the red wallpaper had been changed to match the red carpet, which hadn't even been there before.

All the photos of his mum and dad and Granny Grimstone had vanished from the dresser. The room was empty and soulless, a room for nobody.

A *spare* room.

CHAPTER

8

"What is going on?" Oscar muttered. "Mum!" he cried.

The door swung open, and his mum burst into the room just like he'd summoned her.

She had a candlestick in her hand. Howling, she swung it at Oscar's head.

Oscar just managed to duck out of the way. His mum stumbled, carried forward by her wild swipe, but she quickly turned to face him. Her expression was full of fear.

"Don't you dare steal anything. I've called the police!"

"Mum, it's me! Oscar!"

"Don't call me that! I don't have a son, you villain! You thief!"

She swiped again with the candlestick. Oscar backed away. He wanted to run over and hug her. More than that, he wanted his mum to hug him, to tell him everything was okay. That it all would look better after a cup of tea.

But when he looked in her eyes, he saw only fear, like his mum had never seen him before in her life.

"Get out!" she screamed. "Get out of my house!"

Oscar turned, moving as fast as his crutch would let him. As he bumped down the corridor, he realized that it wasn't just his room that had changed. All the familiar photos were gone, and the furniture had been moved about.

Nothing was the same.

"Get out!" his mum screamed again from the top of the stairs. Oscar heard the triumph ringing in her voice. She'd scared away the monster.

He crashed through the front door and hobbled in a daze toward the road, without any idea where he was going. Maybe he had actually fallen asleep. Maybe this was a nightmare.

Far off in the distance, he heard a siren. Much closer, he saw a tallish figure in a wide-brimmed hat. The figure was standing in Oscar's front yard. The figure's face was muffled by a red scarf, as if that person really didn't want to be recognized.

Oscar jolted. He was so distressed and confused that he knew this was important but he had no idea why. Then a familiar itchy tingle wriggled down Oscar's back. *Phantasma*. The shock was enough to jerk him out of his dream.

As the figure in the hat raised its hand, mist appeared around the person's ankles and curled across the lawn. The pair of shears that Mr. Kenright had left in a wheelbarrow outside of number 32 lifted into the air and flew straight at Oscar's head.

Oscar had no time to move, so he didn't.

He turned ghostly. The shears passed right through him like a guided missile and buried themselves in his front door.

As soon as Oscar looked back at the ghost, all his exhaustion and pain lifted from his body. It felt as if a giant hand that had been gripping him tight had suddenly let go.

Before Oscar knew what he was doing, he bounded forward, raising his crutch like a club.

The figure didn't try to throw anything else at Oscar's head. It didn't try to run either. Instead, from its pocket it pulled out a round object and let it drop from the end of a short length of wire or piece of string. It looked like a watch on a chain—or maybe a yo-yo.

Oscar continued to charge, screaming in rage, fear, and frustration.

But the figure didn't flinch. Instead, it lifted up the object and began to move it very slowly. Oscar could see it wasn't a yo-yo at all. It was a withered eyeball. It was yellowing, crusty with a glowing, bright red pupil moving about. It was alive and it was looking—and as soon as the horrible thing saw him, Oscar stopped.

The scream died in his throat.

He felt a horrible sucking sensation tugging at his soul. He saw bits of his body and his clothes whirling away from him, swirling toward the glowing red eye.

When Oscar looked at his body, he saw the sparkling shimmering light was fading, becoming more see-through, and parts of his fingers were disappearing completely.

The eye was sucking him up! Swirls of ghostly mist were transferring from Oscar's body into the wide pupil of the eye. The eye began to glow.

Oscar panicked and tried turning back to human again to escape. He had the knack now, and it should have been easy, but he couldn't do it right. The ghastly eye gripped him somehow. The front half of his body stayed ghostly and was being vacuumed away. Only the back half of his body turned human. But with the front half of him still ghostly, Oscar could see into the back half, which was still in living form. He could clearly see his human heart beating and his kidneys pulsing and his bloody raw muscles twitching as he tried to run.

Oscar heard a scream behind him. His mum had followed him out into the street—but she wasn't ready for the bloody butchery that she found. Even though she'd been an undertaker all her life, she couldn't handle the sight of half a boy, organs exposed, flailing about on her front lawn.

To be fair, very few people could.

Her scream hummed with terror. It was nearly as good a scream as Oscar's had been, and it was shockingly loud; so loud, in fact, that the eye was distracted for just a second.

It turned to the noise—and the figure turned too.

Suddenly the awful grip on Oscar lifted.

Oscar took his chance. He turned fully human.

Without thinking, he dived forward, trying to tackle the ghost before it could hurt his mum—but his arm and his crutch met empty air. He went straight through the figure without stopping and landed in a lavender bush.

The figure was turning toward him, trying to get the eye to look at Oscar again. His mum was still screaming.

Oscar knew that he was about to die. Later, if you'd asked him why he did what he did right then, he wouldn't have been able to tell you.

In that moment, pure animal instinct took charge of him. He did three awesome things very fast. He turned back into a ghost. He did a backflip out of the lavender bush, landing neatly on his feet. With his ghost strength and whip-quick reactions, he brought his crutch round in a mighty sweep. The crutch connected sweetly with the behatted ghost's stomach. It drove the ghost up through the air, spinning it round like a ragdoll. Then the ghost thumped onto the ground with a satisfying bounce and dropped the eyeball. It burst, collapsing into dust.

Oscar found himself a little startled, staring down at the crumpled figure of his opponent on the ground, with no clear idea how it had gotten there. Oscar's body was twisted round with the force of his blow, his crutch high over his shoulder like a golfer after a mighty drive.

It was his surprise at finding himself in this extraordinary position that allowed the ghost to escape. The ghost reached into his pocket and drew out a lilac-colored doorknob.

Oscar watched in stunned amazement as the ghost turned the doorknob and opened a door in midair. In a flash, the ghost jumped through it, and the door vanished.

His mum was still screaming as the police drove up with sirens blaring. Neighbors were appearing in doorways, woken by Oscar's mom's screaming, and they rushed to help. Oscar's mum was taken inside and given a cup of tea.

But no one noticed Oscar. As a ghost, he was invisible. He followed his mum and his neighbors inside and watched them huddle around the kitchen table. Gary Stevens appeared in the kitchen five minutes later. Whatever satisfaction Oscar had felt at whomping the man in the hat vanished as he listened to Gary talking to his mother about the break-in.

"The thief said he was my *son*," his mum said. "But I don't have a son—though I've always thought of you that way, Gary. Thank you for coming and checking up on me."

"It's no bother, Mrs. Grimstone," Gary said. "You know, I think I saw the thief outside your house earlier. I tried to fight him, but he ran off."

"Oh, you're so brave!" his mum said. "Thanks for watching out for me!"

Oscar wanted to reappear and punch Gary Stevens in the face. But it wouldn't have done any good.

None of his neighbors remembered him. No one told his mum that they'd known Oscar since he was a baby. Worse, the police didn't tell her she'd gone mad. That she had a son, named Oscar, who went to Little Worthington Middle School.

Oscar had been wiped off the map. Obliterated. Erased.

Without a shadow of a doubt, this was worse than any nightmare. It was worse than being actually dead.

Oscar couldn't take it anymore and walked out of his house, with no idea where he should go. He didn't have any other family. He didn't have any friends. And even if he did, they wouldn't have recognized him anyway.

Oscar Grimstone didn't exist.

CHAPTER

9

"Where've you been, Oscar?" Sally hissed. "And get in here now—someone might see you!"

Oscar ducked inside Sally's office and shut the door. He felt like crying with relief. All through his epic journey to the GLE headquarters, he'd been terrified that Sally would have forgotten him as well. It had taken him an hour and a half by train and three night buses to get to West London. He didn't have any money but simply turned into ghost form to get aboard, then turned living again once he was on the inside. As dawn had broken, the shimmering ghost streets of Londinium filled with ghost markets, spreading over the streets of the living city. Oscar followed the river west. When he finally reached the looming stone tower in St. James's Park, he turned living and ducked through a wall while arriving in the lobby past the ghost at the front desk, before flicking back to climb the many staircases to Sally's office. He wanted to give her a hug—but that didn't feel appropriate. He barely knew her, after all.

Oscar settled on smiling—his first smile since he'd left Little Worthington yesterday. He held his crutch close to his chest like a talisman—he hadn't let go of it once.

If his mum knew who he was, she'd have been proud of him. She was always trying to get him to keep hold of his crutch.

"Why are you smirking like that?" said Sally.

"Because you know who I am," Oscar said. "You recognize me!"

"I what?"

"It's a long story. Can I have a cup of tea? Do ghosts drink tea?"

"There'd be riots if we didn't," Sally said. "I'll fetch us both a mug."

Sipping from the small cauldron of sugary ghost tea that Sally brought him, Oscar soon began to feel a lot better. It helped that the tea was piping hot and tasted more or less as it should—though there was a strange dusty feel to the liquid, as if it wasn't actually made with water.

Oscar told Sally about everything: the attack, the fact that his mum thought he didn't exist anymore, his struggle to find his way to London without any money or food or phone. He acted out his finishing blow with the crutch—nearly smashing Sally's jar of boiled sweets in the process.

"I'd never even been on the train by myself," Oscar said. "I had to sneak onto all these buses as a ghost and then turn bodily so I didn't get left behind when it drove off. Nearly got caught twice."

Sally was much less impressed by Oscar's odyssey on the British transport system than by his second encounter with the mysterious hat-wearing ghost. She was positively amazed by the fact that he had defeated it.

"Sharp work there," she muttered. "You're a pretty talented ghost, Oscar Grimstone."

She rootled around in the mess on Sir Cedric's desk and surfaced with a kind of leather strapping.

"Tie this on you—Sir Cedric uses it for his axes, but this way you'll be able to strap your crutch to your back, and keep it on you in case you're attacked again."

"Thank you." Oscar worked out how to put on the harness.

Meanwhile, Sally pulled out her typewriter and began firing off messages to various departments around the Ministry to investigate the attack on Oscar by the ghost with the hat. "We need to track down this Jessie Mur character before he manages to destroy you for good, Oscar," she said. "I'm more and more convinced that he is attacking you because of your special powers. Why else would you be targeted?"

For a few minutes, the office was filled with the machine-gun clatter of her fingers on the keys. Oscar sipped his tea.

Soon her answers started arriving. A cascade of forms and letters appeared out of thin air and landed on Sally's desk.

"Now, tell me again what happened with your mum," Sally said, looking through the papers as they arrived. "It sounds like a memory wipe—but it's not just your mum, is it? It's *everyone*. That's a very difficult trick to pull off. Requires a huge amount of power and top-level organization—only specialists from the GLE Cover-Up team can do that kind of thing."

She held up one of the forms. "But here, look. This is from the Cover-Up team. They say they've done no work since they cleared up the mess you made by the river. No other big jobs have been authorized for over a week. So it doesn't make any sense."

She riffled through the papers. More kept arriving.

"Also, we already knew that the ghost in the hat could poltergeist. It already attacked you once that way, hadn't it?"

"Yeah," Oscar said. "It likes flying sharp objects at my head."

"Not nice," said Sally. "And not easy either. But the ability to poltergeist requires a lot of training. It's not something any ghost can do, and even if you can, you don't get permission to fly mundane objects around willy-nilly. The top brass don't like it—it attracts attention, makes a mess."

"Why would someone learn how, then?" Oscar asked.

"Most poltergeists aren't murderous maniacs. They have applied for a permit and got training in order to complete some unfinished business that is keeping them in the living world—they want to haunt the person who murdered them, or scare someone out of completing an evil plot. Or they want to move an old photo to somewhere their living relative might notice so they feel comforted. It's all very carefully controlled." Sally picked up another paper from her desk. "This message is from the Haunting Department." She held up another form. "They've given no permits for poltergeisting near Little Worthington this year."

"So what does that show?" Oscar said. "Couldn't a ghost just do it by themselves, without permission?"

"Yes, but they'd have to be very important to be taught how to do it in the first place. It's a well-connected ghost that's out to get you. That's why that Ghoul Eye is so worrying."

"It hurt," said Oscar. "Like every part of me was being sucked away."

Sally frowned. "For the GLE, extinguishing ghosts is the most terrible crime there is."

"What was the eye doing?"

"Vacuuming up your phantasma. Killing you. Ghosts only contain a limited amount of the stuff, and when it all goes, it's curtains."

"That's not good!" Now Oscar was worried. "So is half of me gone, then?"

"Don't worry, by now you should have filled back up again. I'm told vigorous exercise gets the phantasma flowing." Sally was still chewing her lip. "But this ghost is much more dangerous than I thought. That kind of extinguishing kit is impossible to find. It's very, very illegal, and you don't just bash it together in your basement. There's only been half a dozen cases of involuntary extinguishing ever recorded. So the ghost that's out to get you is very dangerous and very well connected. We need to be care—"

The office door banged open. Lady Margaret stormed in. She was wearing a canary-yellow gown that showed off her bony shoulders. In her case, they were literally bones.

"Brazen Grimstone!" she snarled. "I see that you've dragged your *unnatural* body back to the GLE. Did you think I wouldn't notice?! You were ordered to remain out of sight at home. There will be consequences. Nasty ones."

She turned her eyes to Sally, looming above her like

she wanted to rip her limb from limb. "And as for you, Detective Cromarty! Helping Grimstone will be the end of you! I will personally ensure that you are sent to the Other Side for this. You will hand in your ba—"

Sally didn't flinch before these terrible threats. Oscar actually thought she was grinning. Lady Margaret noticed this too.

"Why are you smiling?" she shouted. "Don't you realize the trouble you are in?"

"You should look at this," Sally said, holding out Oscar's file, which they'd stolen from the Archive. It was open to his birth-and-death page.

"Do you see who's signed that?" Sally said, pointing.

It's hard for a ghost to turn white. They are already pretty washed-out to begin with—but Lady Margaret definitely turned a whiter shade of pale when she saw the initials MM.

"Looks like Mr. Mortis was happy for Oscar to be the way he is, doesn't it?"

Strange emotions were flowing across Lady Margaret's ravaged face. One of the tendons in the corner of her mouth was vibrating like a violin string. Oscar watched as her terrible anger and her fear of doing the wrong thing waged war.

Sally twisted the knife. "You wouldn't want to go against the direct wishes of the Boss himself, would you?"

"But . . ." Lady Margaret squinted at the signature. "No . . . it's really his handwriting," she said, disappointed. "How did you get this?"

"Contact in the department," Sally lied, so smoothly that Oscar was impressed.

"That's strange," Lady Margaret said. "And you should have gone through the proper channels." Her mouth opened as if she wanted to say more, but the fight had left her. Baffled and broken, like a defeated army fleeing a terrible massacre, she turned for the door.

Sally waited till they heard the clicks of her high-heeled shoes fading down the corridor before she burst into great peals of laughter.

"Did you see her face?!" she crowed. "We got the better of her, all right!"

"Why does she dislike me so much?" said Oscar. "She's a very angry woman."

"Oh, she just hates everything that breaks the rules. To be fair, it makes her quite a good policewoman—wait a minute!"

Sally grabbed her typewriter and dashed off a quick note, her fingers flying across the keys.

"Who's that to?" Oscar asked. "Why the hurry?"

"Lady Margaret's secretary," Sally said. "I'm asking for her boss's diary for the last four days."

"Why?"

"Patience, Oscar—but I think I might have solved the case!"

A few moments later, the secretary's answer appeared on Sally's desk.

"Hah!" Sally said after reading through it. "I knew it!"

Oscar peered over her shoulder, but whatever Sally could see was not immediately apparent.

"Look," said Sally. "You were attacked for the first time two days ago. On Wednesday afternoon. Have a look at what Lady Margaret was doing then."

" 'Three p.m. to six p.m.: Off Duty,' " Oscar read.

"Exactamundo," Sally said. "Now can you see the only other time that Lady M. was off?"

Oscar scanned the page. Lady Margaret was very dedicated. She'd been working more or less nonstop for the last four days. She had meetings day and night, and when she wasn't in meetings, she was going to engagements, or giving speeches, or . . .

"There it is," Oscar said. "Her only time off yesterday was a few hours in the morning."

"Precisely," Sally said. "And when were you attacked for the second time, Oscar?"

"Yesterday morning!" Oscar's mind raced. "Lady Margaret's the ghost in the hat!"

"She certainly might be." Sally nodded smugly. "Think about it. She has the *opportunity*—she was free at those times, wasn't she? She has the *means* too. She's a very power-ful ghost, trained in memory wipes, and has poltergeist-ing abilities as well. I've seen her move cars around with just her mind."

"She sounds dangerous," Oscar said. "But why would she want to kill me?"

Sally looked less certain. "Motive's trickier. Like I said, I think she hates the idea of you existing because you break the rules. Maybe she looked you up in the Department of Records—and now she is trying to get rid of a nasty mess."

"I'm not a mess!"

"Well, you are," Sally said. "But that doesn't mean you have to die. We need to tread very carefully. Get out of here for a start."

Sally scribbled a note to Sir Cedric and hurried Oscar out of the building.

"Sir Cedric's been working really hard for you," she said as they hurried through St. James's Park. "That's what I wanted to tell you when I went to your house. He found a hat shop owner who sold a suspicious ghost a wide-brimmed hat. The ghost said his name was Ernie Hoy."

"Ernie Hoy . . . Jessie Mur. Those are weird names," Oscar said.

"Well, she's hardly going to sign herself Lady Margaret, is she? Come on. Let's go to the pub."

CHAPTER
10

The Shallow Grave was a traditional ghost inn and restaurant. Its secret entrance was on the Strand, tucked between a frozen yogurt stall and an umbrella shop.

Oscar hesitated before he pushed open the low wooden door—he'd never been to a restaurant without his mum before. Of course, Sally sniffed out his uncertainty like a bloodhound.

"Don't worry," she said. "Ghosts won't care about your age. Think about it, you can't tell how old a ghost is from how they look. Take me—I'm more than a hundred ghost years old, but is that how I look?"

Sally didn't look a day older than thirteen—except for her eyes, of course. They were ancient and wise and a little scary, but Oscar decided not to mention that.

They pushed through the door into a cheery fug of conversation and beery stink. The jukebox was playing Elvis. A few other ghosts were watching soccer on a big screen.

"Come on, Busby Babes!" one of them shouted.

"See what I mean?" Sally said, pointing.

Two toddlers were sitting at the bar, with pints of some foaming, shimmering liquid in front of them. They seemed to be discussing horse racing.

One of the toddlers pointed a finger. "If you can't see that Red Rum is never going to lose a Ghost National, then you are the biggest fool I know, Jim!"

"But the ground's hard," said the fattest toddler, who Oscar presumed was Jim. "That favors Desert Orchid."

"The ground's always hard. You ever see it rain in the ghost world?"

"What are you drinking?" Sally said. "Mine's a licorice and apple."

"Ah . . ." Oscar blinked.

Sally pointed at the foaming, bubbly silvery drinks that the toddlers were drinking. One had a candy cane sticking out, and the other looked like it had ice cream bobbling in it. "Ghost shandy," said Sally. "It's made of brewed and infused phantasma. Gives you quite a boost. You can ask for any flavor combinations you like. Just don't get the extra brew."

Oscar thought of the thing he liked the most. "Apple pie?"

The barman frowned for a second, then pulled on a tap. A silvery liquid zipped out, sending up sparkling flecks into the air that fizzed and crackled. Oscar saw a few appley bits emerge from the tap, finished with a slap of cooked pastry that somehow layered itself over the rim of the glass.

Soon they were safely ensconced in a little snug booth off the main bar with the two drinks and a mug of home-made pork rinds. Oscar couldn't help staring wide-eyed at the strange assortment of drinkers in the inn: some, like the toddlers, were naked; others carried swords or pikes or clubs. He saw stiff-starched lace, hippie kaftans, and mysterious robes. One ghost was missing its head, another had a round hole cut neatly in his chest, and at the table next to them a lady ghost was wearing a flowerpot on her head. Many were sitting at tables eating vast plates of extravagant food.

But that wasn't the strangest thing about them. It took Oscar a while to work out what was troubling him.

"Why are they all eating and drinking?" Oscar asked.

"Why not?"

"Well, they don't need to, do they? Do ghosts get hungry?"

Sally shrugged. "Not strictly speaking, no . . . Ghosts don't need anything to survive, except phantasma, of course, but what's better than a hearty meal after a long day's work?"

As Oscar had never had a job, he couldn't answer

that—but he had to admit that his shandy was surprisingly refreshing, even if it had the same dusty, dry feel on his tongue as the tea he'd had earlier.

Something else was troubling him too. "How is the food made, though?" he asked, pointing at a plate of beef being eaten by a ghost wearing a tight bodice with a pearl necklace. "Are ghost cows reslaughtered to make these?"

"We're not that cruel." Sally chuckled. "It's all phantasma. Any ghost can use it to make replicas of stuff from the living world—and the better a ghost's knowledge of what it's creating, the closer the match. So ghosts that were great tailors cut the finest ghost suits, ghost builders build the sturdiest ghost buildings, ghost chefs whip up the most delicious ghost meals. And master ghost brewers"— she took a long, lip-smacking swig of her pint—"make the most refreshing shandies. This was brewed by Gustav 'Three Nose' von Klimt, and what that wonderful Hun doesn't know about brewing ain't worth knowing."

As Oscar and Sally chatted away, Oscar began to feel an unfamiliar sensation. Maybe it was the slight buzz from his phantasma shandy, but suddenly he realized he was feeling decidedly *hopeful*. With Sally on his side, things would be okay. They would get to the bottom of things, together.

Oscar turned to Sally and finally asked her the question he'd been dying to ask.

"How did you die, Sally? And what's it like?"

Sally paused, glass halfway to her mouth.

"That's rude to ask a ghost, you know," she said, frowning.

For a terrible moment, Oscar thought he'd insulted her, just when he thought they were getting on so great. His stomach plummeted into his boots like an elevator with a broken cable. It wouldn't be the first time he'd said the wrong thing. Right now, Sally looked just like how Toby Smith had looked back in history class when Oscar had told him that he preferred putting makeup on dead people to playing soccer.

But then Sally sighed, staring into her fizzing drink. "My dad was a policeman, one of the first detectives in London. I loved his stories and the detective stories I read, and I wanted to be like him."

Sally paused and took a deep swig.

"And then?" said Oscar.

"And then I got a little too involved. My father was investigating Hieronymus Jones, the famous villain. A genius inventor. He started out with bank robberies and robbing jewels from aristocrats. Soon he was smuggling opium and selling guns to anarchists. Blackmail, forgery, rebellion! The whole works. He was the most wanted man in London." Sally's eyes narrowed. "And I was at home that day, when the police messenger came. They'd spotted

Jones in Leather Lane! But Father was out—so I said I'd tell him."

"You went after him yourself, didn't you?"

Sally nodded. "I was foolish. I thought I'd spy on him. Track him down. I thought I'd make Father proud."

"What happened?"

"He shot me with one of his inventions—a harpoon blunderbuss. And laughed as he did it."

Slowly, Sally opened up the top of her shirt. She'd always worn a high collar, tightly buttoned. Oscar had never wondered why till now.

There was a neat round hole in her chest, just below her throat. Oscar could see right through her.

"But that's not even the worst of it," said Sally. "A few weeks later, Jones killed my mother and father too. He diverted a steam train so it ran right into our house. He said he wanted all of us dead, to complete the set."

Oscar was speechless.

"I'm sorry," he said eventually. He wanted to say something more, but nothing seemed right.

"It's okay. That was a long time ago." Sally's eyes left his, darted around the room, and fell, at last, with gratitude, on his crutch strapped to his back in the holder that she'd given him. "How's the strap working out?"

Even Oscar could tell that Sally was trying to change the subject.

"Fits well," he said. "If I ever need to turn living, the crutch will be on hand. I'll be ready next time Ernie Hoy or Jessie Mur or whatever they're called tries to extinguish me in an unusual way." Oscar thought more about it. "And I just don't feel right without it. Like it's not me."

"Yes! That's just it," Sally said. "You're just like the rest of us ghosts. We don't feel right either without our human habits. That's why we hang on to all the clothes and the beer and the pork rinds. That's why we eat and sleep—"

"You go to bed?" Oscar asked.

"I try to catch a good seven or eight hours every two nights. And so should you, Oscar. Sleep keeps ghosts sane and healthy. You've got to remember that the less human you act, the less of your humanity remains. And if you stop sleeping, it takes a big toll: you can slip away from yourself, turn into a shadow, or even a real ghoul, a soul feeder." A shadow passed across her face. "You *really* don't want that to happen. So it's good that you keep your crutch. It is *you*. Have you had it ever since your accident?"

"Well, ever since I could walk," Oscar said. "And Mum always made me take it to school, even when I begged her not to. But . . ."

Oscar suddenly realized something else. Sally had been honest with him. Completely honest.

"Sally," he said. "I'm really sorry."

"It was a long time ago. Don't worry about it, Oscar. You're always sorry."

"No, I mean . . ." Oscar hesitated. Even now he could hardly get the words out. "I am *really* sorry. See, I haven't been telling you the truth."

"At *last*." Sally smiled. "I wondered when you'd get round to telling me whatever it is that you've been hiding, Oscar."

"I'm sorry. I've thought about telling you loads, but it's my biggest secret and I've never told anyone. And—"

"Out with it, Oscar!"

Oscar took a deep breath. "Sally . . . I'm cursed."

As soon as the words were out of his lips, Oscar felt a wave of intense relief, and also more than a little ridiculous.

"Cursed?" Sally asked.

Oscar's throat tightened. At first, the words just wouldn't come out. But then he took a deep breath, and it was like a kink in a hose had been released and it all flooded out of him. "Yes! When I touch flowers, they die. And once, when I fed some goldfish, they died too. Any small life-form gets its life totally sucked out, and the more angry or upset I am the worse it seems to be. And—"

"That's not a curse," Sally interrupted. She seemed *interested*.

"Well, it is a *bit* of a curse," Oscar said defensively.

"Not a bit," Sally said. "You're amazing, Oscar. There

is nothing like you. No human, no ghost. I don't think you realize how special you are. So tell me everything."

Sally had a way of asking questions that made Oscar want to answer, so he did. He told her how he had begun to worry his Curse might have made his dad die. About the bullies who'd tormented him. About everything bad and good that had ever happened to him.

Oscar had never realized how much it helped to share a problem.

They talked long into the night. It was certainly in the top five best evenings of Oscar's life, possibly even top three. Finally, last orders were called. Sally got to her feet.

"Last one. What can I get you?"

Oscar thought for a second. "Chocolate and cornflake."

Sally frowned. "Why would you want corn in a ghost shandy? Honestly, modern tastes. I'm getting a marzipan and mint."

Oscar watched her ordering, and his hopeful feeling returned stronger than ever. Of course, realizing that you're feeling hopeful tends to remind you of all the reasons why hope is a bad idea. In Oscar's case, that meant he remembered his powerful enemies, who liked to blast him with creepy Ghoul Eyes, and his new life-warping, mystery ghost powers, but even all that worrying stuff wasn't enough to chill the warming glow of Oscar's optimism.

Yes, his life had changed in many ways, mostly for the

worse. But one thing was different. And that one thing made almost everything bad worthwhile.

Sally was his friend.

Oscar had never had a real friend before, not *really*. He ran through a checklist in his head to make sure he wasn't getting the signals wrong. Doing that kind of thing was one of the reasons Oscar didn't have friends. He did it anyway.

For one, she laughed at his jokes, even when they were bad.

She seemed interested in what he had to say. She didn't say he was crazy. She didn't call him the Death Dork, or the Four-Legged Cripple.

Although she definitely thought he was odd, she hadn't thrown rocks at him.

She wasn't pretending to be his friend in order to stick mean messages on his back with Post-it Notes. This was what had happened the last time Oscar thought he had a friend, three years ago.

Most important, Oscar got the distinct impression that Sally actually liked him. Oscar wasn't very good at judging this, because it hadn't really happened before. But it felt true.

Sally returned with the drinks. "But get these down us quick. Five minutes until closing."

"But we need to go through the case some more."

Sally smiled. "You're a marvel, Oscar—tight-lipped for days and then, once you've started, you won't stop. But after all that nattering, it's time for bed, don't you think? I need some sleep and you don't want to turn into a soul feeder."

"Can I stay with you?"

"No, better you stay here. It's safe—and my house might be watched by Lady M. The GLE have records of where their workers live. If she's the one who wants to get rid of you, she might ambush you in the night. No way you can escape being extinguished if you're in cuckoo land. Here—I'll get you a room."

She paid the barman for a room for the night with a strange assortment of currency—a gold florin, a couple of shillings, and some modern pound notes—that she pulled from her purse. The barman gave Oscar his key and pointed toward the stairs.

Before he went up, Sally gave him a hug.

"Don't worry too much, Oscar," she said. "We're going to sort all this out."

There was no doubt in her voice.

Oscar grinned. It was good to feel hopeful.

It was even better to have a friend.

Dutifully, Oscar did as he was told.

He opened the door of his room with a crooked iron key. The room had a thick carpet and heavy furniture. An old coal fire glowed without any heat in the grate. He turned on the gas lamp by his bed and fiddled with the chunky old-fashioned television. It was showing reruns of old shows from the seventies. He tried the bed. It was springy and did not creak. The pillows were soft.

He undressed and found that if he kept his crutch and shoes close enough to him, they stayed ghostly and didn't fall through the floor. He stowed them under the bed and climbed in.

He looked around and realized there was no ghost bathroom.

Oscar found himself wondering if ghosts still had to use the toilet or brush their teeth. Maybe there were some parts of being alive you were happy to let go of when you died.

He turned out the lamp.

In the thick, soft darkness, he found himself wondering about a lot more things. It was very hard to go to sleep. Not just because his brain was pinwheeling about inside his head, Oscar felt like he'd actually forgotten how to be tired. Sleep was a distant dream.

He was worried about his mum. He was worried about being a ghost forever. He was very, very worried he was never going to go back home. What if his mum was stuck not remembering him? What if Jessie Mur or Ernie Hoy or whatever that criminal in a hat was called had messed with her mind permanently? What if they came back and used the mist to kill her, to try to draw Oscar out?

After fifteen minutes alone in the darkness, Oscar sighed and turned on the lights again. The records that they'd taken from the Archive were on the bedside table. Oscar began to flip through them. If he couldn't sleep, he might figure out what was going on. Maybe he'd see something that Sally had missed.

He reached for his dad's file. His hand shook a little as he turned the first page, and then he started to read and forgot all his worries. It was amazing. He felt like he was getting to know his father for the first time.

Even better, his dad was awesome. Julian had grown up—just like Oscar—in a funeral home—but unlike Oscar, he'd had loads of friends and done well at school and even had trials to play soccer for Arsenal. But he hadn't taken it up, because he wanted to help his mum—Oscar's awesome granny—who'd run the funeral home all by herself all that time. Reading through, Oscar kept on hoping that he might find out who his grandfather was, but that was the only thing that wasn't in the file.

The story of how Oscar's parents met and fell in love was very romantic. She was working as an optometrist, and his dad had gone in for some new glasses. There was an extract from Julian's diary in the file:

She was looking at me through these big, goggly glasses— and I saw her eyes and I knew that I wanted to spend the rest of my life with her. . . .

Oscar felt a bit embarrassed about reading the next few pages, so he skimmed his parents' courtship and the early days of their marriage. There were a few photos in the file. They both looked so blissfully happy.

Suddenly, Oscar couldn't take it anymore. The fact that his mum couldn't even remember any of this made it much worse. He snapped his father's file shut—whoever had done the wipe on her memory had killed his father again.

He'd never really realized it before, but the time that you *really* die is when no one alive remembers you. No one remembered his dad anymore but him.

He looked at his own file.

No one remembered him either. That meant Oscar was dead. He opened the file—and flicked through it. Although he knew it all already, he had a sneaking suspicion there must be something, somewhere, that they were missing. There must be a reason.

It wasn't a fun read. Unlike his dad, Oscar hadn't had a full, or happy, life. He'd spent most of his time in his room, moping. It was heartbreaking, really.

Oscar read on. At last, he came inevitably to the torn back page. His death page.

He ran his finger over the sliced edge and was just pondering if a ghost could get a paper cut, when his hand brushed over something else. Something he hadn't noticed before.

The back leaf of the file had small, looping indentations etched deeply into the thick cardboard. Oscar blinked at them for a second, trying to work out what might have caused them. It looked as if someone small, like a mouse, had gone ice-skating across it—or maybe like . . .

Oscar gasped.

He ran over to the fire and scrabbled about in the grate until he found a piece of soft charcoal. He wasn't quite sure that this would work. He'd seen it done once in a *Scooby-Doo* episode, which was hardly reassuring.

He fully exposed the gray back leaf of the folder. He took a deep breath. He knew he'd only get one chance.

Slowly, carefully, he began to rub the charcoal over the cardboard.

Like magic, writing appeared on the page. But Oscar's joy was short-lived. He couldn't help reading Mr. Mortis's flowery handwriting as it was revealed, and by the end, his tears were smudging the charcoal.

> *Addendum to Contract*
>
> *I, Mr. Mortis, bear witness to the bargain made today by Julian Grimstone. I declare that his life is forfeit, and in return, I grant new life to his son, Oscar, who should have died on this day. Julian Grimstone will die in his place.*
>
> > *Signed,*
> > *Mr. Mortis*
> > *Julian Grimstone*

Oscar's father's signature was crisp and firm and certain. As if he had no doubt what sort of a person he was.

In a daze, Oscar checked the back of his father's folder. It was just the same: the charcoal revealed a second, duplicate contract scratched into the cardboard.

But even as the words appeared, Oscar's mind wasn't there. It had been transported back to a dark country road. It had been an icy night, his mother had said once. A hard frost and a sharp corner.

He saw the car's wheels spinning, upside down.

His father and Mr. Mortis had made the bargain, somehow. And then with the horrible bureaucracy of death, Mr.

Mortis—the Grim Reaper—had written that bargain down twice, his pen pressing so hard he'd scratched it right into the cardboard beneath. He'd made it official. He'd made it happen.

Oscar saw his father standing by the burning car, signing away his life.

He imagined the little baby boy in the wreckage starting to cry as his father fell to the ground beside him.

Oscar's heart broke.

It should have been me.

CHAPTER

11

It was a long night.

In a daze, Oscar read through every page of both files, scanning as fast as he could. He went quicker through his own file, which was rather dull, as he had already discovered. His father's was three hundred pages long, but there was a useful index at the back for key moments, and a timeline at the start with a summary. There was nothing in either file saying that Oscar's Curse had killed his father. Oscar found himself wondering why the files didn't mention his Curse at all. But it didn't matter. Oscar's dad was dead because of Oscar. Why had Mr. Mortis allowed them to switch? There must be some clue. Anything that would help make it right.

But there was nothing. Just more reminders of the many ways that Oscar squandered his father's sacrifice by not living life to the fullest, by locking himself away on his own the whole time.

When morning finally arrived, Oscar needed to turn back to his human self again and feel alive. His dad had sacrificed his own life so Oscar could keep his. He wanted to appreciate it.

He left word at the pub, in case Sally came to find him. Then he turned into his living form and went out into the living city of London.

As soon as he turned bodily again, crushing tiredness and hunger smacked him hard in the face like a brick in a sock. His bad leg ached. But Oscar didn't mind. His dad had died just so that he could feel this awful. He was damned if he was going to give it all up by becoming a ghost.

He crutched slowly to the nearest human café. He had just enough real change in his pocket to buy himself a decent breakfast. The kind of breakfast his dad had loved. The bacon was good, but the tea tasted like golden nectar. The real thing just couldn't be beat.

Oscar was finishing his second pot when Sally staggered in. She didn't bother to pick her way around the other tables and breakfasters but walked right through them as if they weren't there. She was weighed down by a large leather-bound tome about the same size as a suitcase.

"Morning, Oscar," she said. "You get some sleep? You look like death."

Oscar wasn't really in the mood for jokes.

"Rough night," he said. "It's hard to sleep."

"Got a present for you. It's the official biography of Mr. Mortis. Sir Cedric suggested that I get it out from Records. He figured there might be something useful in here, maybe an explanation for why he's taken an interest in you. You like books, don't you? Fancy a read?"

He pointed to the gargantuan text. "Every page?" He'd done enough reading last night.

"Sure. Wish I could have a piece of your bacon."

Oscar suddenly become aware that people in the café were staring funnily at him. To them it must have looked like he was talking to thin air.

"Let's get out of here," he muttered. "Got something to show you too."

Back in Oscar's room, Sally was utterly gobsmacked by what Oscar had discovered. As Oscar's story unfolded, her mouth dropped open and stayed that way.

"Lawks!" Finally she found her voice. "Mr. Mortis *personally* brought you back from the dead, Oscar! Do you know how crazy that is?"

It wasn't crazy. It was awful.

"But why did my dad have to die?" Oscar asked bitterly. "Why couldn't Mortis just save my life if that's what he wanted to do?"

"Oh, no." Sally held out her hands like a set of scales. "The balance of life and death, Oscar! It has to be maintained. There're rules. Big, *important* rules. If they get broken, the whole world might break down. That's Mr. Mortis's main job, to make sure that people die when they are supposed to. But this switcheroo! I've never heard of anything like it. It breaks every rule there is."

Sally had to sit down, and she began to talk it all through, what it meant, how it could happen, the reasons behind it. Her mind was still whirring away, her thoughts tumbling over one another like a basket of cats in a clothes dryer. Oscar watched her grimly—he'd feel a lot better if she didn't seem so excited. This might be interesting and intriguing for her, just another revelation in the case—but this was Oscar's life.

"We have to show these to Sir Cedric! He might know if this has ever happened before. Though I don't think it has, or has it? No. Why did Mortis intervene? What's so important about *you*? I don't even think it's possible. Golly! What a mess." She gathered up the papers and stuffed them in her bag. "Great detective work, by the way. You should be a ghoul, Oscar."

A quick coach ride later, they arrived at the Department of Contraptions. Oscar felt full of energy in his ghost form, and it made him feel guilty; he shouldn't enjoy the ghost world so much. His dad had died so Oscar could live. But for now, Oscar had to stay a ghost to find out the truth.

It didn't help Oscar's guilt that the Department of

Contraptions turned out to be the best place he had ever been in his life . . . or death.

The entrance was right beneath the flashing neon signs in Piccadilly Circus. But within ten seconds of passing through the small, unmemorable door, Oscar had completely forgotten about that famous London sight. It was long gone, along with every reasonable, rational thought in his head.

"What do you think?" Sally asked him.

He tried to say something, but it all got mixed up and then mashed together in his mind, so that all he could manage was "Urg."

"That isn't a word, Oscar," Sally said. She patted him on the back. "But I think it nicely sums it up."

There'd been a lot of mind-frying revelations since he became a ghost, but the Department of Contraptions was like plunging your brain into a deep fryer.

"Impossible, eh?" said Sally, grinning.

They were standing on the very edge of an enormous . . . hangar. The roof was somewhere above them, *maybe*, but the building was so big it actually seemed to have its own weather system. Funny clouds were floating high above, lit up by strange flashes of light and distant explosions. The air was thick with the greasy feel of phantasma.

"What's that?" Oscar asked, craning his neck back to look at the monstrous pink airship that was hanging from the ceiling above them. But sitting within the gigantic space of the Department of Contraptions, the ship looked like someone's forgotten birthday balloon.

"Oh, that's the Party Zeppelin." Sally shrugged. "The Ministry of Ghosts' summer bash is really something."

"But what is this place?" Oscar asked.

"Well, some ghosts, rather than using their dead lives to carry on doing whatever they did when they were alive, decide to come up with the craziest inventions they can think of. The Department is where they work and experiment together. But there is also a Restricted Property office, where all the illegal or dangerous contraptions are stored. Things like phantasma-sucking devices, for example. We can see if any have been checked out."

"Right. Brilliant."

"Try not to gawk too much—we've got a long way to walk."

It was hard. Everywhere Oscar looked, he saw all kinds of wonderful stuff. Dancing cows swooped above them carrying messages on their horns. Sally explained that these had been created last week by a Life Maker—someone who creates afterlives for the Other Side at the Department of Afterlives—on his day off.

Sally showed Oscar the Zonomorphs, the weird clanking machines that Life Makers used to craft their afterlives. They looked a bit like a cross between a steam train, a windmill, and a very fancy oven. A huge battery of them was set up just inside the door, and they were belching out purple smoke as Sally and Oscar walked past.

In the distance, giant revolving letters changed color and spelled out inspirational slogans like *Die Better!* All sorts of ghosts were coming and going through doors that popped out of nowhere. There was a cheerful bustle to the place.

Despite everything that Oscar had been through, he couldn't help smiling.

"In here, the Ministry can keep an eye on the inventors and make sure they don't release anything dangerous into the real world. Because everything's powered by phantasma, you can dream up some pretty odd ideas."

As Sally and Oscar continued into the enormous warehouse-like room, a small, floating personal chandelier began to hover over their heads.

"Restricted Property," Sally said to her chandelier.

The chandelier glowed pink and swung away to the right, leading them on into the maze. They walked past or through dozens of inventions in the works. Oscar's favorite was a room full of vehicles: some were like the carriage that brought them there, others were more modern motorbikes and cars, and then there were the machines that looked like they'd been put together inside someone's dream. A giant baby with wheels. A fishcopter. A rocket-powered rocking horse.

In another room, ghosts were flying about, all working together to build an enormous sculpture of Queen Elizabeth I. It seemed to be made out of individual grains of rice, painstakingly hand-painted.

"Why?" Oscar asked.

"Why not?" Sally said. "It's only taken them thirty years. Pretty quick work if you ask me."

After an utterly jaw-dropping fifteen-minute walk, their chandelier guide brought them to the heavily guarded entrance.

Intimidating guards armed with scary-looking weaponry like giant mechanical fly swatters and bowling ball throwers that hummed with phantasma checked Sally's credentials before letting them inside.

"These guys are new," Sally whispered. "Not sure if I like 'em."

Beyond the entrance was a dark, gloomy cave. Various pieces of confiscated machinery were piled haphazardly about. A clerk with an extremely bored expression sat at a table in the back. His face brightened considerably when he saw that he had visitors.

"How may I help you kids?" he asked. "Here to find out about the naughty stuff, eh?"

"I'm Detective Sally Cromarty. I'm from the Ghouls," Sally said, flashing her badge again. "I want to know if any ghost has signed out equipment for channeling or storing energy in the past few months."

The clerk's smile vanished. He dragged out yet another huge leather-bound record book. He licked his finger and began to page slowly through it.

"Never in a hurry, are they?" Oscar whispered.

"Lots of empty time," said Sally. "Got to fill it somehow. Come on, have a look at this stuff!"

She took Oscar on a tour of the confiscated contraptions. She showed him sticks of dynamite and piles of plastic explosives that, when detonated, gave off a powerful shock wave of phantasma that could tear ghosts apart; a catapult that threw samurai swords; a pair of goggles that could see into vaults; and a real skeleton key made of bones that could open any ghost doorway in existence.

"Those tools were used by the Kray twins. Me and my dad helped catch them forty years ago. Proper pair of villains, they were."

Oscar found himself drawn to a complicated piece of machinery in the corner of the room. It had brass valves and odd handles and a wonderfully ornate gear system. It looked like a clock for turning time inside out.

"What does this do?" he asked, reaching out and running his finger over the frame.

"It's for counterfeiting coins, I think," Sally said. "Wait! Do you hear something?"

With a hissing sigh, the machine sprang to life. Cogs churned; steam vented. A deep, groaning noise issued from somewhere deep inside.

"What did you press?" Sally hissed. "Stop it!"

"I didn't press anything," said Oscar.

With a rattling roar, a torrent of golden sovereigns started vomiting from a funnel in the side of the machine.

"Stop that!" the clerk screamed. "That's dangerous!" He sprinted over and started heaving on various levers. Cogs clicked and whirred. Gradually, the coin torrent slowed to a trickle and then stopped.

The floor was now covered in a small lake of coins. A fortune.

"Can I clean these up?" Oscar asked. "I'm very sorry."

"Don't touch *anything*!" snapped the clerk. "And I'll do it."

The clerk opened a door in the air with a key he pulled from his pocket and hauled out a vacuum cleaner. He started vacuuming up the coins. Sally and Oscar got out of his way.

"He's right, you know," Sally said. "You'd better not touch anything, specially that dynamite. If that goes off . . . Pff, wouldn't be much of us left."

"But I didn't press any buttons! Or levers . . . or anything."

"Exactly. You just stroked it, and it sprang to life. I saw."

"Oh," Oscar said, still a little puzzled. "So what happened?"

"*You* happened." Sally's eyes were shining with excitement. "Normal ghosts can't do that. Your phantasma is very, very powerful. Remember the reading we took of you on the phantasmagraph in the mortuary—it was off the scale. These machines are powered by phantasma, and your phantasma caused it to go haywire. Think! That was just one touch! Imagine what you could do with the proper training!"

The clerk sucked up the last of the coins and put the vacuum cleaner back in its invisible closet.

"I'd just gone through the book, when you had your little accident." He sniffed. "There's only been one high-level access recently."

"Oho!" said Sally. "What did they take?"

"Funnels, a Hungry Bottle, and a Ghoul Eye," he said. "I remember them because they didn't say anything and they were covering their face with a hat and a scarf."

"That's our man," Oscar said.

"Or woman," Sally said. "Did they leave a name?"

The clerk ran his finger down the list. "Yes. Ren Simons."

"Hmmm . . . That's another name that could be a man or a woman," Oscar said.

"Yep." Sally was chewing her lip. "Doesn't help us much. Except they took a Hungry Bottle. They are very, very dangerous." She turned back to the clerk. "And was this 'Ren's' paperwork in order?"

"Do you think I would have let them take a Hungry Bottle if it wasn't?" shot back the clerk, bristling.

"Of course not." Sally smiled pleasantly. "And thank you for your patience."

"Sorry about the coins," Oscar added.

They made their way back, guided by their flying chandelier.

"This is really bad," said Sally. "Only someone with the tippy-toppest level of security clearance could take a Hungry Bottle."

"Well, who could that be?"

"About seven or eight ghosts in London," Sally said.

"And is Lady Margaret one of them?" Oscar asked.

"Yup!" Sally nodded. "She's fishy as a ferret. We have to tell Mr. Mortis! But how can we? What was it? A forty-year wait!" She pounded her fist in her hand. "We have to find a way to see him. Jump him somehow."

A door suddenly opened in the air in front of them, and a lady ghost stepped out pushing a ghost baby in a stroller. The baby was talking on a phone attached to a teddy bear.

"We'll need to meet an accurate assessment of the operational parameters before we can give the go-ahead," the baby snarled. "And I don't think Morrison will like it."

Normally, Oscar would have been fascinated by such a crazy sight, but he hardly noticed. He'd stopped dead in the corridor with a funny, faraway smile on his face.

"Toddle on," Sally said, turning when she realized he was no longer with her.

Oscar didn't move.

"I think I've got an idea," he said.

CHAPTER
12

"Are you sure about this, Oscar?" Sally asked out of the corner of her mouth. "You can still back out."

"No," Oscar said. "I mean, yes, I'm sure, and no, I'm not backing out."

"I mean it. This is a bad idea."

They were hurrying down the final oak-paneled corridor at the top of the Ministry of Ghosts headquarters. Again, they'd made it through all the barriers, until only the last—Mr. Mortis's terrifying secretary—remained.

"What's the worst that could happen?" Oscar said, trying to sound brave.

"Oh, that's easy," said Sally. "The worst is you plummet three hundred feet to your actual death on the pavement. You'll look like raspberry jam."

"Welp. Too late now," Oscar said.

The secretary had seen them coming. Her smile was so chilly it could have frozen lava.

"I told you to come back in forty-one years," she said. *"Yesterday."*

"We wanted to check if you'd had any cancellations . . . Moira," Sally said, squinting at the badge on the secretary's chest. "We're optimists, see?"

"How quaint. Let me assure you there have been no— Hey! *HEY!* What do you think you're doing!" the secretary shrieked as Oscar took off running.

He was past her desk in a flash, feet flying.

The secretary was stunned only for a moment before she pressed her alarm button. A siren started wailing. The two enormous security guards appeared from their cubbyhole. They moved quickly, like agile mountains, and blocked the way.

Oscar didn't swerve to avoid them. He ran faster. The two giants grinned.

Just before he crashed into them, Oscar turned bodily.

The guards grunted in astonishment as he passed right through their ghostly bodies.

A moment later, Oscar turned back into a ghost and ran on down the corridor. Behind him, he heard Sally cheering.

Ahead was a heavy mahogany door. The brass plaque on it read:

MR. M. MORTIS
MINISTRY HEAD

Oscar didn't bother opening it. He used another trick—flashing bodily for a second and then back to ghost. But this time his feet were about to fall through the floor when he switched back, so he tumbled headfirst into the office and rolled across the carpet.

From his hands and knees, Oscar surveyed the room. It looked rather ordinary considering whose office it was. A large desk dominated the space. It had a heavy book on it and an old-fashioned quill pen. Various houseplants were dotted around the walls. Several shelves were filled with a collection of novelty mugs.

Oscar could hear someone muttering, but from his position on the floor, he couldn't quite make out what was going on.

He raised his head. It looked, unless he was very much mistaken, as if a ghost—a male ghost in a tweed suit—was whispering into a cupboard. Was that Mr. Mortis?

Oscar blinked and looked again. He couldn't put his finger on it, but there was something oddly familiar about that cupboard.

Before he could think what it was, the door slammed open and the security guards tumbled into the room, closely followed by Sally and the secretary.

The ghost jumped away from the cupboard as if he'd been stung.

"What is the meaning of this?!" he fumed. Oscar recognized the flustered features of Sir Merriweather Northcote, Mr. Mortis's right-hand ghost. His cheeks were flushed, and his comb-over had fallen over his wide, glistening eyes. The small, plump man pushed out his chest and went to still the pocket watches that were swinging from his rumpled jacket.

Everyone spoke at once.

Security was bellowing for Oscar to get to his feet.

The secretary was apologizing hysterically for her failure.

Sally was congratulating Oscar on surviving.

"Where's Mr. Mortis?" Oscar shouted. For some reason, his voice silenced everyone.

"Away in Fiji," Northcote replied. "Urgent business called him away." He laughed mirthlessly. "Left a big mess behind. I've had to step into the breach—a lot to be looked after. Population up means more people dying. It's a simple equation, really."

Northcote had recovered his composure impressively quickly.

"What business?" Oscar asked. "Why Fiji?"

"He chose to go on a work trip to Vanua Levu," Northcote replied, as if that was obvious and all that needed to be said. He tapped his nose with his finger and winked. "You'll keep that info hush-hush, won't you? It's best that no one realizes I'm running the show in his place."

"I'll bet," Sally said.

Northcote smiled thinly. "A tough job, but someone's got to do it."

"You're doing very well, sir," the secretary chimed in. "Death rates are going down under—"

"That's very kind of you, Moira," Northcote cut her off. He frowned slightly. For the first time, he seemed to realize just how strange the situation was. "How did this awkward pair get past you, eh? Some damn foolery, I'll bet."

Oscar was again impressed by how quickly Northcote had seized control of the room. Despite his short stature, he seemed to double in size as he strolled toward them. He checked three of his watches, sighed, and put them away.

"I'm not sure, boss," the Viking muttered sheepishly. "Ran right through us."

"We can take them away," the sumo wrestler said. "Do you want to put them in jail?"

"That won't be necessary, lads. Mr. Grimstone, and Detective Cromarty, I am a very busy ghost. You have already wasted too much of my time—but I suppose you must have some very important news if you were that desperate to see Mr. Mortis. So tell it to me. Quickly."

"There's a senior ghost running amok, sir," Sally said. "She's twice tried to murder Oscar. She used a Ghoul Eye—and she's got her hands on a Hungry Bottle too."

"A *Hungry Bottle*?" Northcote said. "That's a serious accusation. Are you sure?"

"Quite sure, sir," Sally confirmed. "She must be stopped."

Northcote started pacing, his brow furrowed. "Well, it's clear that Lady Margaret must devote more resources to the problem." He thrust a finger decisively in the air. "We must act and act quickly."

Oscar and Sally exchanged glances.

"That's just the problem," Oscar said. "It's Lady Margaret who's doing the attacks."

Sir Northcote didn't stop pacing but skipped a step.

"Impossible," Northcote said. "Implausible. Lady Margaret is one of our best and most capable ghosts. I can't believe she'd turn rogue. You must be mistaken."

"Sir, the evidence is quite damning. You see—" Sally started to explain, but Northcote cut her off.

"No, no, I will take it from here." He sighed dramatically. "The work never ceases, does it?! Moira, send out a mass summons to the Board. We meet in an hour. Get right to the bottom of this." He pulled out another of his watches. "Work! Work! Work! So much to do! So little time!"

With the two giant security guards looming over them, it was clear the interview was over. They escorted Oscar and Sally in no friendly fashion out the building and into the busy street. The sumo wrestler barreled Oscar and Sally to the ground with a jolt of his huge belly, and the Viking gave Oscar a final slap on the back of the head for good measure.

For a moment, they stayed seated on the sidewalk. The living walked through them, while ghosts gave them curious glances. As Oscar finally stood up and dusted himself off, he wasn't really sure if they had succeeded in doing anything at all.

"Fat lot of good an inquiry will do," Sally said as Oscar pulled her up. "We need to talk to Sir Cedric. I trust him and he'll have a good idea. Always does."

They climbed into Sally's carriage. She grabbed her typewriter and fired off a quick message to Sir Cedric.

"I'll ask him to meet us at my house," she said. "We need to update our case board."

Sally's house was even messier than it had been before. She left Oscar in the sitting room while she went to get some tea and biscuits.

"Have a look at the board—see if you recognize any patterns," she told Oscar. "You're good at that kind of thing." She'd updated it last night—there was a picture of

Oscar stuck to it, and one of Mr. Mortis and another of Lady Margaret. Around Lady Margaret there was a little spider's web of string, and a collection of scribbled theories about why Lady M. might want Oscar dead.

She is a sniveling old fusspot who doesn't like people who don't fit in with the rules.

She wants to steal Oscar's powers.

She wants to use his powerful phantasma to make powerful machines. And/or blow up the Department of Contraptions because she sees the head of the department as a rival to becoming junior secretary to Mr. Mortis.

She wants to cover up Mr. Mortis's switch with Oscar because otherwise other ghosts might ask to swap places with the living.

None of them seemed very convincing. Except maybe the first.

Another section had a list of the various pseudonyms that the hatted assassin had used: *Ren Simons, Jessie Mur . . .* Oscar picked up a pencil and scribbled in *Ernie Hoy.* That didn't seem to make anything any clearer.

Oscar's eyes wandered and landed on a tattered piece of paper poking up on the other side of the board from Sally's other case—the one about her parents. He remembered Sally's story at the Shallow Grave inn about Hieronymus Jones. How the mad inventor and criminal killed Sally, then her parents. It seemed a long time ago.

Feeling a little guilty, he turned the board around. This side of the board had scientific reports about ghouls, various descriptions of Hieronymus Jones's cunning disguises, and a whole section devoted to the strange weapons that Jones had invented. Right in the middle was his Wanted poster.

Hieronymus Jones had a nasty smirk.

"Who are you really, Mr. Jones?" Oscar asked the photograph. "Hieronymus is a funny name. Is that why you turned bad? Were you bullied?"

There'd been a few funny names recently, Oscar thought. Hieronymus Jones, Ren Simons, Jessie Mur, Ernie Hoy.

As he glanced over Sally's board, he started repeating the names over and over in his head. They fit together well—they had a pleasing rhythm on the tongue.

Hieronymus Jones, Ren Simons, Jessie Mur, Ernie Hoy.

He was looking at a picture of a ghost that had been extinguished, when something cracked inside Oscar's head. He stopped, blinking.

"Hey!" said Sally, coming into the room. "You're not meant to look at that."

Oscar ripped the Hieronymus Jones poster from the board and snatched up his pencil.

"Hey!" said Sally—she sounded genuinely furious, but Oscar didn't care. He scribbled the names down, pressing so hard he tore the paper.

Hieronymus Jones, Ren Simons, Jessie Mur, Ernie Hoy.

"Do you see?" Oscar asked. He couldn't keep the excitement out of his voice. *"Do you see?"*

CHAPTER

13

"I can't . . . believe you figured that out." There was something odd in Sally's voice. It wasn't anger at least—which was a relief. Oscar couldn't help but feel that he'd done something wrong.

She was staring wide-eyed at the paper in Oscar's hand.

The letters of all the fake names that the assassin had given were hidden inside the name Hieronymus Jones.

Oscar had checked it over. He wrote out *hieronymus jones* three times, putting each letter used in the aliases into capitals.

hIERONyMuS joNeS
REN SIMONS
hIERonyMUS JonES
JESSIE MUR
HIERONYmus jonEs
ERNIE HOY

"It can't be a coincidence," Sally murmured, eyes wide. "It just can't."

Oscar tried to make her laugh again. "The advantage of having no friends is that you have to have hobbies. I like puzzles. Probably too much." He pointed at the sheet of paper. "It's like a Russian doll of aliases! Don't you think it's like he wanted us to notice?" Oscar asked. "I mean, why choose names that are just like your own, unless you wanted to give us a clue?"

"Typical. That's just his style—the monkey-faced twazzock—" Sally stopped herself from saying something worse. "Always thinks he's cleverer than everyone else. Always getting away with it. Always *smirking*." She crumpled the poster savagely, as if she couldn't bear to see his face.

"Are you okay?" Oscar asked, a little taken aback.

Sally was swaying slightly, and her eyes weren't focused. She looked like she was about to have a heart attack, or maybe explode.

All of a sudden she didn't seem like a policeman at all. She looked just like a normal thirteen-year-old girl who was hurt and angry and a little lost. Oscar wanted more than anything to help her.

"You all right?" he asked, rather uselessly.

"No. I'm not." Sally ran out of the room. Before Oscar could stop her, she had climbed into her carriage and driven off.

Alone in the street, Oscar had no idea what to do. He felt awful. She'd needed his help, and he'd failed her.

"You always make things worse, Oscar," he said to no one.

This didn't make him feel better.

He was just turning to go back into the house, when he saw a flash of light. Ahead, he saw Sir Cedric come whizzing down the street on the back of a giant ostrich with a siren strapped to its head.

Oscar had never been pleased to see anyone in his life.

Even better, once Oscar had explained everything as best he could, Sir Cedric guessed where Sally had gone immediately.

"A bad business," he muttered as he hauled Oscar up. "Luckily, it's a nippy beast, your ostrich! Took this from GLE transportation. We need to move fast! Remember to hold on tight—and grip with the knees. Right, lad, tallyho!"

Oscar didn't need telling. He was gripping Sir Cedric's armored waist as firmly as he could. A galloping ostrich was a bumpy ride indeed.

Happily, they didn't have far to go, and as soon as they arrived, they saw Sally's carriage parked crazily across the pavement.

The sign above the door read *Paranormal Rehabilitation Unit.*

"Evening, Gladys," Sir Cedric said to the receptionist—a meek-looking ghost surrounded by Persian cats. "Would you happen to know if Sally is visiting?"

"She got here not long ago," said Gladys. "She's seeing the two patients now. Poor lass. Seemed in a right state. Wouldn't even say hello to Mr. Tiddlemas." She held up a particularly fat cat, which purred.

"Hello, Mr. Tiddlemas," Oscar said.

"You're a nice boy," Gladys said.

Somewhere upstairs, someone started screaming. The teeth-rattling howl set Oscar's hair on end. Mr. Tiddlemas hissed and bared his teeth.

As Oscar and Sir Cedric went up the stairs together, other screams started up, answering the first. The cries twisted and twined round each other, like a dreadful choir, or a pack of demon wolves on the hunt. They sounded *hungry.*

"What is this place?" Oscar said. "What are they?"

"This is a hospital," Sir Cedric said. "And those are real ghouls—feeders. I think they can smell you coming."

They saw Sally standing in a long corridor. She was leaning against a thick metal door, peering through a small glass window.

As they came closer, she punched herself in the head, quite hard.

"Hey, Sally, stop!" Oscar said.

But she didn't. A frenzy seemed to have gripped the detective.

"He's done it again," she muttered. "And you've missed it *again*, Cromarty. Again and again and *again*!" She punctuated each word with another thump to the head.

Sir Cedric grabbed her wrists.

"Sally! It's okay. You're okay. We're okay!" Oscar was shocked to see that she was crying. The howling was all around them. It was horrible.

"Look at me!" Looking into her eyes, Oscar at last got her to see him.

"Why does Hieronymus Jones want you?" Sally asked. "What did *you* do?"

"I don't know," Oscar said. He preferred not to think about it. "But it's not your fault."

"It is," Sally said. "It's always been my fault. Look at them!"

Oscar glanced through the little pane of glass and gave a gasp of shock.

He saw two figures in the padded cell. Their eyes glowed red. Their mouths were black holes surrounded by sharp white teeth.

As they howled, they tore at the walls with their claws.

"Those are my parents," Sally said.

She slumped down against the wall, still holding the poster twisted up in her fingers.

"What do you mean?" asked Oscar softly.

"See, I didn't tell you the whole truth either," Sally said.

"That doesn't matter," Oscar said. "Not a bit."

"It does." Sally swallowed hard and pointed at Hieronymus's smirking face. "He killed my parents twice."

"What?"

"He killed my ma and pa once back when we were alive," she said. "And then when we were ghosts, we tried to catch him. So he tortured them. He sucked out their phantasma—but not enough to kill them. Just enough so they turned into . . . *that*." She jabbed her thumb in the direction of the padded cell. "*Soul feeders*. Real ghouls."

Sally frowned. "He did it for fun, laughing. Just to get back at us. He's done it to loads of people. Not enough to kill them but enough to make them hungry forever. He's a *monster*, and I swore that I would catch him—but now he's laughing at me again. And I've failed. I failed you. I failed my parents."

Oscar didn't know what to say. Sally looked so small and scared and alone. So he bent down and gave her a hug.

"Thanks, Oscar," she said. "You're a pal."

"We'll get him," Oscar said into her shoulder.

Sally laughed. "I've been saying the same thing for a hundred years. Fat lot of good I've done."

"That's not true." The hug continued.

Oscar was starting to worry. Although starting the hug had been pure instinct, he had no idea how one went about ending these things. He'd never hugged anyone who wasn't a blood relative before. He'd certainly never hugged a girl his own age (give or take a hundred years). He tried patting Sally on the back as an experiment.

Sally didn't seem to notice Oscar's confusion, or mind the patting.

"Someone once told me about a book. They said I reminded them of this mad captain from the story who was dead set on killing a whale. Apparently the maniac chases the beast all over the sea until he finally gets his chance. And then the whale kills him."

"I think it's called *Moby-Dick*," Oscar said.

"You read it? Is that how it ends?"

"No idea." Oscar grinned. "It's about a billion pages long. Anyway. Let's go catch your whale."

By the time they'd gone back down to Gladys and the cats, Sally had calmed down. Her good mood continued for precisely three seconds. That's the time it took for a message to appear in midair and thump against her chest.

"What's it say?" said Sir Cedric.

"It's a summons," said Sally, scanning the text. "Lady M.

wants to see us at Ghoul headquarters. She doesn't sound very happy."

"When does she ever, the pencil-pushing renegade?" Sir Cedric said, mounting his ostrich.

Everything had been removed from Sally's office. Her mounds of notes and her comic books had been cleared away. Her desk was empty.

"They've even taken my bin." Sally's mouth settled into a grim line as she pointed out where the trash can used to be. "There's going to be murders."

"I smell Lady Margaret's hounds." Sir Cedric sniffed. "They've taken my kettle. Someone will burn for this!"

"I hope you don't do anything stupid, Sir C," Sally said. "Because I plan to."

"Steady on," said the knight. "I wouldn't want you to get hurt."

"I would," snapped Lady Margaret, storming into the room. Her hair looked even more magnificent than usual. Her scowl even more menacing.

Sally didn't quail. "So you've made your move," she said. "Villain! Tell me: What did Hieronymus offer you? Was it money you wanted? Was it power?"

Lady Margaret blinked—and then growled as the

meaning of Sally's questions became clear. Her eyes burned with a terrible anger.

"How dare you?!" She took a step toward Sally.

Oscar was suddenly conscious of how sharp Lady Margaret's nails looked, almost like the talons of an eagle.

Sally didn't flinch. "How dare *you*?!" she shot back. "Traitor! Liar!"

The only nostril that Lady Margaret still had flared. "You have ignored my direct orders. You have run about London with this monstrous boy. You have stolen records from the Archive—did you think I wouldn't check? And now you have broken into Mr. Mortis's private office, and it seems you have the flaming gall to accuse me of collaborating with Hieronymus Jones himself!"

Eyes popping, raw tendons flexing, dramatic hair flapping—she looked like a wicked witch from a story, or an avenging demon from a movie, or just about the most terrifying sight Oscar had ever seen. He took a step back.

With vicious, cobralike speed, Lady Margaret's claws went for Sally's eyes.

GONNNNG!

Sir Cedric moved with surprising speed for a ghost in full plate armor. He stepped in front of the blow and caught it on his chest. Any ordinary person would have broken their fingers on Sir Cedric's breastplate, but Lady Margaret's wiry digits bounced off with a *clang*.

"Tread carefully, Your Honor," Sir Cedric warned.

Lady Margaret snarled. For a moment, the ghost looked as if she was considering taking them all on, ripping them all to shreds. Then she unclenched her hands.

"Thanks, Sir C," Sally whispered.

"You're all finished!" Lady Margaret said. "Done. It's over. Give me your badges. Now." She clicked her fingers, and GLE officers stomped into the room.

"You can't do that!" Sally said. "You're guilty." She began to yell, turning to the other officers. "Listen to me! The chief's working with Hieronymus Jones! She's betrayed us all!"

"Lies!" Lady Margaret snapped. "Wicked lies of a desperate ghost! If you do not hand over your badges now, I will have your visa revoked and you will be forcibly moved on to the Other Side! You too, Sir Cedric! Give them to me now."

The grim-faced ghost officers looked eager to carry out her orders.

"We can't fight all of them, old fish," Sir Cedric muttered. "Best to do what she asks, eh?"

He rummaged inside his armor and brought out his badge.

"Proudest twenty years of my death, serving the GLE," he said as he handed it over.

Sally flung her badge in Lady Margaret's face. "You'll regret this."

"Oh, will I?" Lady Margaret smirked. "I think you'll find you're finished. Your sad little story is over. I think you'll cross to the Other Side tomorrow. A failure in life. A failure in death. Pathetic."

She turned from Sally and pointed a bony claw at Oscar. He could see her tongue working through her jaw. It looked like an eel, hiding in a crack, waiting to pounce.

"Grimstone. You are a monster. You have no visa. You do not belong here in my world. If I see you as a ghost again, I will assume you have made a choice. Go back where you belong, or die. I will send you to the Other Side in a speedboat. Have I made myself clear?"

CHAPTER

14

"Wait!"

Sally was walking so fast that Oscar and Sir Cedric couldn't keep up. She stormed out of the GLE tower in a blind fury, striding through St. James's Park while muttering terrible threats.

Oscar had to grab her by the shoulder to get her to stop.

"Leave me be!" she snapped. "I'm going to climb on that boat and cross over to the Other Side. Be done with it! Be done with this. Curse that treacherous witch!"

"Sally, you must not do that," called Sir Cedric, hurrying to catch up. "When Mr. Mortis returns, he will sort anything out. He always has answers. Remember the soul feeder invasion!"

"He won't know. He won't care. What was he thinking? Going off to Fiji!"

"I'm sure he had his reasons," Sir Cedric said.

Acid fear was bubbling through Oscar's veins as he saw

what Sally was threatening. Right now she was his only friend in the whole world. She was all he had.

"You can't give up," he said. "You can't leave us."

"Watch me," Sally said, turning to go. Her anger was furnace hot, burning away everything else.

"But I don't exist in the other world," Oscar said. "Someone even wiped me from my mom's memory. Don't you see? I can't go back!"

"So cross over with me," said Sally. "I hear it's nice on the Other Side. You can see your dad at last."

They had reached the river. Up ahead, Oscar could see the dock for the giant bone ship. The huge funnels were pouring out smoke. The ship's horn bellowed like it was signaling the end of the world.

"No, Sally!" He grabbed her sleeve. "Stop this! You can't let Lady Margaret win! You're better than that. What would your dad want? He was a detective, wasn't he? He'd want to catch the crook!"

Sally looked like she wanted to argue, then stopped. Slowly, she looked from Oscar to Sir Cedric and back again.

"You're bloody right," she said.

"I am?" said Oscar, a little shocked.

"So he is," Sir Cedric said. "Sound common sense from the lad. Detective Simon Cromarty was a top cop."

"I'm being a fool," Sally said. "I'm doing just what that evil witch wants, like an idiot!"

"Yes!" Oscar said. "I mean, no! You're not an idiot, but you're right, that is what she wants."

"I need to fight," Sally said, ignoring Oscar. "We need to fight. But how?"

"Like King Henry's men at Agincourt!" Sir Cedric punched the air. "The odds are stacked against us. But that will not matter with truth on our side!"

Oscar cheered. He briefly wondered if Sir Cedric was actually at the battle of Agincourt, and maybe even died there—that might explain the armor. The knight's words shook with real feeling.

"Well said, Sir C!" Oscar cried, hoping to pump Sally up. "They won't be expecting it! We'll counterattack. We'll give them both barrels! A double broadside!"

"Have at it!" Sir Cedric struck a pose. "We'll storm them on the beaches! We'll fight them in the halls! They will taste our British steel and fall back like the cursed swine they are!"

Oscar had a feeling that this was laying it on a bit thick. Lady Margaret would certainly be expecting them to try something, but he didn't want to jeopardize Sally's new optimistic spirit. He felt energized by their enthusiasm too.

"We will never surrender!" he shouted, rather wildly. Being a bit mad felt rather good.

"That's right, Oscar!" Sally was grinning too. "Hah! Now, if we're going to war, we've got to act fast but carefully. All the case files are still back at my house. I'll fetch them; then we can meet back at the Shallow Grave inn. Make a plan for our victory. We gather the evidence, lay it out, then take the evidence to Sir Merriweather Northcote, or some big brass at the Ministry. But not before we put a tail on Lady M. and catch her in the act."

"I'll stow my gear and free my fists," said Sir Cedric. "When do we rendezvous? Teatime? I'll bring my sharpest sword."

"Teatime," agreed Sally. "Oscar, you are very much in danger if you are seen—so keep your head down, all right? Stay in your room in the inn. We'll come and fetch you, and we can discuss how we're going to win."

"I'll bring you a rapier," said Sir Cedric. "Might serve you better than those crutches."

And without further ado, Sir Cedric and Sally were gone. Oscar was left alone in the street, wondering what exactly had just happened.

He didn't dawdle for long. The memory of Lady Margaret's threat was still fresh in his mind. He set off toward the inn—or at least in the direction he hoped was the pub.

He kept a careful watch—ignoring the hustle and bustle of living London was second nature. He hardly saw that now. But Londinium was just as alive. He passed apothecaries and children playing, ghosts eating lunch in cafés and all manner of old-fashioned vehicles from pedal cars to tanks. By St. Paul's Cathedral, he hurried past some builders raising an extension to the phantom church in the graveyard. From inside the cathedral, a ghost choir was bellowing out a hymn.

Their sweet voices followed him down the road. It sounded sad and ancient and not a little eerie.

He turned back, trying to listen to the song, and that's when he saw the familiar hat.

It was bobbing through the crowd. It was wide-brimmed and dark gray, and it was about twenty yards away.

It was definitely Hieronymus Jones again.

Oscar quickened his pace, but in the mirrored glass of the building he saw that the hat was moving faster too.

Oscar crossed to the other side of the road, watching carefully.

A figure stepped out of the crowd and followed him across. It was wearing the hat and the scarf, and carrying a large gray bag. The bag looked lumpy, as if it had a lot of heavy equipment in it.

Oscar started to run, dodging ghostly carriages and cars. As a ghost, he could move like lightning. He built up enough speed that his feet left the floor, wheeling just above the pavement and road. He even used a cart to springboard over a row of market stalls.

"Watch it, mate!" He narrowly avoided being trampled

under the hooves of a shimmering stallion after he landed. Jones followed, pounding after him, never losing ground.

Oscar ducked sharply into an alley, but he didn't fool Hieronymus Jones.

Oscar could hear Jones's gear clanking in his bag. It sounded like heavy sheets of metal banging together.

But despite all that weight, Jones was as fast as Oscar. Faster even.

Oscar was getting worried now. He didn't think he could outrun Jones.

Still sprinting as fast as he could, he burst out of the alley into a main road. He took no notice of the living cars and taxis that were driving through him. Looking around, he searched desperately for a way to get out.

Surrounded by speeding traffic, Oscar saw a real-world bus pulling up at a bus stop. An idea sparked just as Hieronymus Jones emerged from the alley. He stopped when he saw Oscar was waiting for him.

"I know it's you, Hieronymus Jones!" Oscar shouted, stalling for time. A few ghost heads turned in alarm. The name was infamous.

But Jones said nothing. He was reaching inside his coat. Oscar stared at him, trying to see his eyes. They were shining darkly under the brim of his hat.

"I know you're working with Lady Margaret," Oscar said. Out of the corner of his eye, he saw that the last few human passengers were getting on the bus. This was going to be very close.

"We're going to finish you," he said, trying to waste more time. "We're on to your game. We know what your plan is!"

More ghosts were watching and pointing now, wondering what was going on. Oscar could hear them muttering to one another.

"What's all this?!" a tall ghost in a top hat shouted. "Is that Jones?"

Hieronymus Jones pulled a brass funnel out from under his coat. As the coat flapped open, Oscar saw the glass bottle the funnel was connected to. It looked as if the bottle was strapped to his chest. A weird darkness throbbed inside the glass container.

"He's got a Hungry Bottle!" Oscar shouted. "Run!"

Panicked screaming broke out around him, but Oscar stayed very still. It took all his courage not to run. He was still watching Jones's eyes, which twinkled, as if he was smiling.

The brass funnel was pointing straight at Oscar. Jones's finger pressed down on a button.

Right then, in the real world, the bus started to pull away from the bus stop.

Too late. Oscar felt an emptiness inside him and his energy draining away as the Hungry Bottle started to suck his soul out in a stream of shimmering mist. It was a horrible, shredding feeling—and if anything, more powerful than when the Ghoul Eye was used on him. More and more of his phantasma was leeching away, rushing toward the brass funnel.

Out of the corner of his eye, Oscar saw the bus heading right for him.

He took a deep breath and jumped in the air as high as he could. The brass funnel followed him, sucking away. He was still watching Jones's eyes—so he saw the surprise bursting inside them like a firework, and then the anger, as Jones realized what was going on.

The bus accelerated forward. Oscar turned bodily and was caught neatly by a seat in the back of the bus.

Luckily there were no living people near him when he appeared out of thin air. He sat down and waved goodbye to Jones as the bus carried him away.

It took Oscar another hour to circle back to the inn. He was very careful now, and rather weak. But he couldn't stop grinning.

Part of that was fear, of course—fear mixed with a healthy jolt of adrenaline. He tried not to imagine what would have happened if he had timed his jump even a little bit wrong. He could see the Headlines.

MYSTERY BOY IMPALED ON SEAT INSIDE BUS

Or maybe:

BUS HORROR AS BOY APPEARS INSIDE ENGINE

No one would have known who I was, thought Oscar. *My mum doesn't even know she's my mum.* But even the chilling reminder that he didn't exist wasn't enough to dampen his elation.

He ran up the stairs two at a time, practically dancing, burst through his door, and, still grinning, bounced down on the edge of the bed.

Oscar wondered if this was how superheroes felt after they did something amazing. He'd been about to die, but he'd nailed it. Hieronymus Jones was the nastiest ghost around, and Oscar had escaped him yet again.

He wondered if superheroes got tired of being awesome.

Oscar certainly hadn't.

Even though it had been a few hours, there was still no sign of Sally or Sir Cedric. As a way to pass the time, Oscar began to page through the giant biography of Mr. Mortis that Sally had left in his room.

It wasn't the kind of book that you just picked up. For one thing, it was as heavy as a block of cement, but it was actually pretty interesting for a three-thousand-page tome. For another, the first parts of the book were written in languages that Oscar didn't even recognize. As he turned the pages, he wasn't even sure if it was writing he was looking at. It looked like tiny squiggles drawn by beetles more than something you'd read.

Oscar gathered enough to see that Mr. Mortis has been around since the beginning of time. Although it seemed like he hadn't always been called that. He'd had many different faces and names. Flicking through the book, Oscar saw pictures of Mr. Mortis with a dog's head, or a strange two-faced crown, or old-fashioned Greek robes. There were even pictures of Mr. Mortis where he wasn't a Mr. but clearly a Mrs.

Even so, for all the different faces and costumes in the book, all of them had something in common. It was something in the eyes, and the set of the eyebrows. A flash of humor, a dash of wisdom. A gentleness.

Oscar supposed you'd need that if you were a god of death. He also couldn't shake the feeling that he'd met Mr. Mortis before.

He turned to the back of the book, hoping to find something written in English. Eventually, flicking through, his eye fell on this passage.

Latterly, Mr. Mortis, while human in appearance, remains the embodiment of death. His existence ensures the force of death remains in the world. If he ceased to exist, no one would die anymore, which would be extremely problematic. Luckily, Mr. Mortis has been around for a very long time and has no plans to cease to exist, though some theorize it is possible that his energy could be extinguished. . . .

Oscar thought the forces of death sounded a bit like his own abilities. Didn't he have the power to kill things when he touched them? Maybe he had a death force inside him?

But before he could wonder any more about that, he turned the page. And what he saw there drove everything else from his mind.

Oscar was staring at a picture of Mr. Mortis. He hadn't seen one properly until now. This one was in modern dress and very recent. As in all the others, he had the same gentle expression and hint of a smile in his eyes, like he was remembering a good joke. But it wasn't that that made Oscar gasp.

His hands were trembling. It felt as if the world had suddenly turned around him and gone *click*. Everything made sense.

He knew why he was the way he was.

He knew why Mr. Mortis had saved him.

It was a golden, toe-curling, hair-frying, mind-buzzing feeling. He was right. He knew it!

Oscar started to laugh.

CHAPTER

15

"Do you see?" Oscar asked. "It's not a coincidence, is it?"

Sir Cedric took the dog-eared photo of Oscar's father and laid it next to the picture of Mr. Mortis in the book. The knight had turned up at the inn an hour after Oscar, carrying files from GLE HQ that could help with the case—he'd even managed to snag Lady M's personal file from a contact in Ghost Resources. Sally still hadn't arrived from her house, where she must still have been gathering files.

"Laddie, there's no denying it," he murmured. "The same long nose, the same high forehead. Those wide dark eyes and a widow's peak! They are practically identical. By gad, sir, Mr. Mortis is your grandfather!"

Oscar could hear the wonder in Sir Cedric's voice.

Oscar could still feel the same wonder himself. His mind was buzzing with ideas—of course it explained a lot, but then again, there were so many more questions now that needed answers.

Like: What happened if the God of Death was your grandpa?

Suddenly, Sir Cedric dropped to one knee and bowed his head. "It is an honor, my lord."

Now Oscar felt embarrassed. "No need for that."

"I owe fealty to the offspring of my liege lord," Sir Cedric said, still kneeling. "It is your due."

"Don't think many living people would agree with you about honor," Oscar said. "My mum always told me it was a real scandal when my granny had a baby when she wasn't married. She never admitted who the father was to anyone—not even my dad. I suppose that all makes sense now."

"Living people do get judgmental about these things," Sir Cedric agreed. "Small-minded. Such things matter so much less when you are dead."

"I don't know," Oscar said. "The god of death isn't an ideal boyfriend, is he?"

Sir Cedric chortled. The laugh echoed hollowly inside his helmet. "On the contrary, he is the greatest boyfriend you might wish for. And this explains a lot about you, young Oscar."

It did. If Mr. Mortis represented death in the world,

that certainly explained why Oscar killed flowers when he touched them.

The genetic lottery. Some people got blue eyes or a good memory from their parents. Oscar got the power of death.

It also explained why Mr. Mortis had made that extraordinary agreement with Oscar's father and broken all the rules just to keep Oscar alive. Oscar didn't know how he felt about that choice. His grandfather had allowed his son to die to save his grandson.

Oscar couldn't really bear that thought. The chance he'd been given.

"I won't waste it, Dad," he muttered. "I promise."

Sir Cedric was watching him carefully.

"My lord," he began.

"Don't call me that," Oscar said.

"My lord," insisted Sir Cedric, "shall we go see where young Cromarty has got to?"

It seemed terribly odd that Sir Cedric was deferring to him.

"Very well," Oscar said.

It took half an hour to ride by ostrich to Sally's small ghost house in Mile End. Oscar felt very conspicuous as they galloped through the streets, but no one took any notice. That was a good thing about ghost life—everything was so crazy that you could blend in pretty easily. Sir Cedric kept an eye out for GLE patrols, but they didn't see any ghosts out looking for them.

Someone had come looking for Sally, though.

Her red door was hanging off its hinges, shattered. It looked as if it had been punched in by a giant fist.

"By Mortis's beard!" Sir Cedric exclaimed, a wobble of shock in his voice.

They ran inside. Oscar was desperately afraid.

"Sally!" he shouted. "Sally!"

The usual cheerful mess of Sally's house was a now a broken bomb site. There were signs of struggle every-where. Drifts of paper were strewn about, and Sally's modest possessions were smashed or tumbled out of drawers.

She hadn't had very much. A few sticks of furniture. A few jars of sweets. A dead rubber plant.

"Sally!" Oscar shouted, running up the stairs. There was no answer.

When he came downstairs, Sir Cedric was kneeling on the floor, sifting through the papers.

"This is your case file, my lord," he said. "I wonder what was taken."

"Apart from Sally, you mean." Something horrible oc-curred to Oscar. "What happens to a ghost's body when it is extinguished? Does it disappear?"

"If Sally had been extinguished, there would be a residue, my lord," said Sir Cedric carefully. "The process is quite messy. I do not believe that happened here."

"Here," Oscar said. The knight's implication was clear. It might be happening right now, somewhere else. "Where has Jones taken her?"

Sir Cedric shook his head. "Do you think it was Jones?"

"Look," Oscar said. He picked up a gray cardboard folder. It was his death file that they'd taken from the Archive. During the struggle, some ash had spilled across the floor from the grate and someone, stepping in it, had left a dirty, great footprint across the file.

"Whoever owned this shoe is the one who took her," Oscar said. "Funny kind of shoe. It's a bit pointy."

"So it is," Sir Cedric said. "Might I have a look, my lord?"

Oscar was about to hand over the file when he noticed something else. The dirt and soot from the bootprint had uncovered another bit of ghost writing. Writing that Oscar hadn't noticed the first time. It was easy to see why: the writing was very small and precise, printed in a neat bureaucratic hand that was quite different from Mr. Mortis's extravagant flow. It was on the bottom part of the folder, just below Mr. Mortis's signature. He turned the page to the light and read.

"Hang on," Oscar said. "So Northcote was there at the accident? When it happened?"

"That is his signature," Sir Cedric said. "So it would seem so."

"But he said he had no idea about any of this! That means he was lying. He knew who I was all along, and he didn't say anything!"

"Deuced odd," said Sir Cedric. "Dammee!"

"It's more than odd," said Oscar. "It's suspicious. What if he's the one behind all this?"

"*Northcote?*" Sir Cedric asked. "Are you sure? The man's a withered prune."

"I'm positive," Oscar said, surprised at how certain he felt. "He's always complaining about how he doesn't get any credit. How he does all the work. What if he's done something to Mr. Mortis and wants to take his job? That Fiji story was awfully fishy. And Northcote could easily use his clout to get Hieronymus Jones all that gear. They must be in league!"

"A dangerous and deadly ally," said Sir Cedric, but he was nodding along. "You see things truly, Oscar. But that still doesn't explain why he would want to kill you."

"No, it doesn't. I'm not worth the bother, am I?"

"Ohoho! Yes, you are, my lord!" Now it was Sir Cedric's turn to have a good idea. He slapped two metal fists together. "Perhaps he wants to kill you because you have Mortis's blood flowing in your veins? Perhaps your very existence is the only thing keeping him from achieving total power? It is potent, you know, your inheritance. You're the last thing he needs to tidy up. It's the kind of detail that Northcote wouldn't miss."

That felt true to Oscar—and more than a little scary. Northcote had a really good reason for killing him—Oscar was the most powerful ghost in the world.

Sir Cedric was already striding out of the house.

"Wait!" Oscar said. "Where are you going?"

"To stop him, of course," Sir Cedric said, climbing up on its back. "And to save Sally. Keep up, my lord."

Once Oscar climbed in, Sir Cedric was away. He drove the ostrich hard, whizzing through London at breakneck speed. The crutch strapped to Oscar's back made it awkward to sit on the bird, but there was no way Oscar was leaving it behind.

"Every second counts," Sir Cedric growled. "Sally is in terrible danger."

It took them only seventeen minutes to arrive at the Ministry. This must have been some kind of record, Oscar thought. Sir Cedric had ridden like a lunatic—half the time, the ostrich had been almost flying, threatening to tumble over. He'd taken such risks that Oscar had shut his eyes for the last five minutes of the trip.

It was only when the ostrich had come to a complete halt that he dared to open them again.

"All right," Oscar said, staring up at the imposing Ministry building. "So now we go back there? Back up to Mr. Mortis's office?"

"Precisely, my lord," Sir Cedric said. "You have hit the nail on the proverbial tombstone. We will go there, and we will confront the villain Northcote."

"How are we going to get inside? Won't they have guards?"

"We have right on our side." Sir Cedric stood tall and jutted out his chin. In his armor, he looked the very picture of a noble knight.

Then he bent down toward Oscar and tapped a finger on his helmet, just where his nose would have been. It clanked softly.

"Also, I know a cunning way in," he whispered. "Helped build the new extension a thousand years ago. Know all sorts of secrets, my lord."

"That's handy," Oscar said.

Sir Cedric's cunning way in turned out to be Mr. Mortis's private staircase. It wound up through the heart of the building, and it was utterly unguarded. They climbed stairs for a long time. Sir Cedric whistled "Rule, Britannia!" all the way.

At the top was a secret door hidden behind a portrait. Sir Oscar looked out through the picture's eyes and scanned the room.

"Good," he said. "There's no one there."

Oscar couldn't help feeling that this was all a little easy, but he wasn't complaining. They made a quick search of the office. Sadly, Northcote hadn't left any incriminating documents behind. Oscar was a little disappointed—in his mind's eye he'd imagined a little folder with *MY EVIL PLAN* stamped on it in red letters. It seemed like the kind of thing that Northcote would do.

"What now?" Oscar asked. "Do we wait for him to show up? What about Sally?"

Sir Cedric was searching through the garbage bin. "He will return, I'm sure of it."

Oscar wandered about. This didn't feel right. He was missing something.

His eye fell on the cupboard in the corner of the room. Suddenly, he remembered Northcote standing beside it and whispering. When he reached for the handle, he felt a familiar cold tingle and a shiver ran down his spine.

He *had* been missing something. There was *phantasma* here.

Oscar examined the handle. It looked wrong for the door—too big—and oddly familiar.

Oscar blinked at it for a moment. Where had he seen it before? He pictured Hieronymus Jones pulling a handle out of his pocket. He saw him use it to open a door in mid-air and escape. This was the same one, he was sure of it.

"It's only a handle," he said as he turned it.

The door creaked open on an impossible space. Ancient stone stairs led down into the darkness. A cold wind blew up from the depths. The air smelled of dank and decay and great age. There was a faint sound of humming machinery too.

He turned with a smile, ready to share his discovery.

"Loo—"

Sir Cedric hit Oscar in the face with the wastepaper basket. The blow sent Oscar reeling.

What'd he do that for? he thought, until he was hit with the truth.

Sir Cedric was a traitor.

Then his feet went out from under him. Rolling backward, he tumbled down the stairs into the darkness.

CHAPTER

16

Tumbling down the stairs didn't hurt as much as Oscar was expecting. He slammed his head into the wall three times. Somersaulting, he crushed his spine repeatedly on awkwardly shaped steps. He even whomped himself twice in the nose with his own kneecap.

If he'd been alive, he'd probably be dead. Instead, he was just in agonizing pain. Oscar hadn't realized ghosts could feel pain until now.

Crumpled at the bottom of the stairs, Oscar looked about him. Or tried to. He'd never seen stars before, but he was seeing them now, tiny bursts of pain that exploded behind his eyes like pinprick fireworks.

From what he could see, the cavernous room looked a bit like a crypt from a horror movie. It had cobwebs and moss-eaten statues and sinister, pointy arches. At the same time, it looked just like a mad scientist's laboratory. At the end of his tumble, Oscar had narrowly avoided impaling himself on a propeller-powered one-person plane. Every surface he could see was crammed with bubbling retorts, Bunsen burners, blunderbusses, brass cones for extinguishing guns, bombs, and brains in jars. A giant mechanical robot suit loomed in the darkness.

Near the stairs, he spotted an incongruous everyday touch: a hat stand with a long coat and scarf and a very familiar, wide-brimmed hat.

Hieronymus Jones.

"Oscar! What are you doing, you fool?" Sally's voice shouted.

Oscar blinked and looked toward the noise.

"Wake up! Run! While you've still time!" Suddenly, Oscar realized that the statue he'd thought he'd seen on the far side of the crypt was actually Sally tied to a pillar. Northcote was lurking in the shadows beside her, watching him.

"I was wondering when you would show up," the villain said with a wry smile. "Didn't expect you so soon, though."

Still a bit dazed, Oscar didn't reply or get to his feet. He was staring at the tall, unconscious man tied to the pillar next to Sally's. The man was wearing a suit. He had neat black hair flecked with gray. There were many brass funnels pointing at him, and loads of complicated piping. The air around him hummed with energy, as if a storm was about to break.

"This . . . is your grandfather," Northcote bellowed with glee, as if he was revealing a grand secret.

"Mr. Mortis," Oscar said. "What are you doing to him?"

"My goodness!" Northcote exclaimed. "Not even a flicker of surprise. You've worked it out already, haven't you? Not bad, Oscar!"

The piping that was connected to Mr. Mortis was slowly sucking phantasma from him. The air wobbled around him. It stank. A strange, briny chemical smell. Oscar could see that the pipes were connected to several large bell jars, which were all full of a dark, frothy substance that seemed to writhe as he watched it.

Behind the machine was a huge shelf filled with little glass jars neatly labeled with people's names. The jars glinted and swirled darkly—the same awful frothing.

Phantasma, Oscar knew at once. All those jars! A lot of ghosts must have been extinguished here.

"Oh, and to answer your question, Oscar, we are killing your grandfather." Northcote giggled, as if he was surprised at his daring for saying such a thing aloud. "Problem is, it's taking rather longer than we thought. Huge amount of phantasma stored up in him, you know. He is a deity, after all."

Sir Cedric clanked past Oscar. He had a brass trumpet in his hand.

"Traitor!" Sally snarled, trying to shake herself free. "Villain! Snake!"

Sir Cedric struck her in the face with a mailed fist. Sally moaned. Then Sir Cedric pointed the brass trumpet at her face.

"Do what we say, Oscar. Or Sally dies." The plummy, cheerful knight had vanished. The voice that had taken its place was a cold, calculating sneer.

"Don't listen to him," Sally said. "Everything he says is a lie."

"Who are you?" Oscar said.

"You haven't guessed yet?" Northcote said. "Tsk, tsk, Oscar."

Sir Cedric flipped up the visor on his helmet. At once, Oscar recognized the face from the Wanted posters. It was Hieronymus Jones himself.

He was smiling.

"How did you get the boy here without a fight, Jones?" Northcote asked.

"Oscar saved me a lot of trouble by working everything out," Jones said with a shrug. "I just had to *nudge* him a few times. Made it all very discreet. It'll be much easier to dispose of the lad down here, in private, than out in Londinium. Perhaps we can harvest him too?"

"Bravo," murmured Northcote, rubbing his hands together. "We're nearly set, then."

"Why?" said Oscar, getting to his feet.

"What do you mean, 'why'?" Northcote asked.

"Why are you doing all this?"

"For the good of the Ministry," Northcote said. "The fact is, I do all the real work: the administration, the mountains of paperwork! If you had any idea of the hours I put in while Mr. Mortis loafed about and took all the credit. It was a very inefficient system."

"Sounds like it's for the good of Northcote," said Oscar. He was trying to sidle round, grab something, anything that could be used as a weapon. There were several jars of Mr. Mortis's phantasma on a table near the plane. Oscar remembered Sally in the Department of Contraptions saying you could use the stuff as a bomb. That made sense. The jars were giving off a ripe, chemical stink that was practically alive.

"That too, my boy. That too. I *deserve* to be in charge after all my hard work. And Mortis was never going to retire. He had to be helped."

"You're both as bad as each other!" Sally shouted. "When this gets out, you're finished!"

"Finished?" Northcote said. "We're just getting started."

"*We*," Sally said. "Listen to yourself. You're teaming up with *Hieronymus Jones*."

Oscar wondered if Sally had realized what he was trying

to do. She was certainly trying to distract them. He took another couple of steps toward the loaded, stinking jars.

"It made perfect sense," Northcote said. "I needed to kill Mr. Mortis, and it turned out that Hieronymus here had been working on a plan to do *just that* for twenty years. That's why he disguised himself as Sir Cedric. *Deep cover.* Such admirable dedication to villainy."

Oscar sidled another few steps.

"You're idiots," said Sally. "Extinguish Mr. Mortis and you kill Death. That means no living person will ever die! There'll be chaos. The world will end!"

"That's right!" Hieronymus grinned. Oscar could see the madness in his eyes. "No more new ghosts—and the living world will fall apart! Win-win!"

"And fewer ghosts means less work for me! We'll come out smelling of roses!" Northcote's eyes were glazed and wild, and he kept fiddling manically with one of the watches hanging from his jacket. Oscar remembered what Sally had told him once, how ghosts can become fixated from doing the same thing, over and over, for hundreds of years. They could lose perspective. But Northcote had done more than just that. He'd gone completely insane.

The two ghosts cackled. Oscar was happy for their good humor to go on. He'd nearly reached the glass jars. One more step and he was there.

"Hold it right there, Oscar." Jones's voice lashed out like a whip. "Don't think I haven't noticed what you're doing. Move again and Sally gets it."

Oscar froze.

"Don't listen to him," Sally said. "Do— Aaaaaargh!"

Sally started screaming. Jones had pressed the button and the trumpet was starting to hoover her up.

"How interesting," Northcote said, watching her die. "These weak ghosts vanish so terribly *fast*."

"Stop!" Oscar shouted.

Sally was growing faint already. Oscar couldn't bear it. "Stop!" he screamed again. "Kill me instead! That's what you want to do, isn't it?"

"No!" Sally sobbed, but her voice was very faint.

Jones pulled the trumpet away from Sally and advanced on Oscar.

"I'll make this easy for you," he said. "Just close your eyes. It'll be nice and quick."

"Promise me you'll let her go," Oscar said. "Untie her!"

"You have our word," Northcote said. He started working Sally free from the ropes that bound her. "As a gesture of good faith, I will release her too. There's something poetic about this. Your father did the same for you. Such a noble sacrifice. Quite *heartening*, when you think about it."

Sally slumped to the ground, mumbling something. She

was hardly there at all, so faded that barely a shadow remained.

Oscar didn't close his eyes when Jones raised the trumpet. He watched. Even though it hurt. It hurt worse than anything he had ever experienced before.

The awful shrinking, shredding feeling tore bits of him away. With a kind of dumb horror, he watched worms of phantasma wind out of his body. His phantasma was a lighter color than Mr. Mortis's—a kind of pearly gray, with bursts of iridescent light curling inside it—quite beautiful, really. It twisted out of his body and whooshed up into the trumpet. The awful jar that Jones was carrying around his waist filled quickly.

Oscar could smell himself dying. A raspy gasoline stink. His vision grew dark.

He began to fade. He fell to his knees, and then his legs gave way and he slumped to the floor. He tried to hold on. He had to save himself for as long as he could.

He was getting thin now. Thin and stretched and the sucking, ravenous hunger never stopped gnawing him away.

He might have been screaming, but it was hard to tell. His ears were long gone.

Jones, very far away, gave a *tsk* of disgust. He'd filled the jar and needed to change it for a new one. The sucking stopped.

It was glorious.

It was like an angel had suddenly appeared and taken away all of Oscar's pain. He lay there, watching Jones methodically unscrew the Hungry Bottle and turn to find a new one.

This was the moment he'd been waiting for. With the very last scrap of himself that remained, Oscar drew his crutch from where he'd kept it strapped to his back, trembling with the effort. It felt good in his hand.

It felt right.

This is mine. This is me.

Northcote shouted something, but Oscar couldn't hear anymore because he didn't have any ears. He could hardly see either—but he could smell. The stench of Mr. Mortis's jars was like a beacon.

Oscar lashed out as hard as he could. The crutch connected solidly. The glass smashed. Dark ghost energy spurted into the air. Most of it fell straight onto the engine, which roared to life with a deafening scream.

The blast of air splintered the remaining phantasma into a fine mist. It sprayed on Oscar, and his strength rushed back. Suddenly, he felt better than he'd ever felt before. The rush was overwhelming—a wave of good energy that drove everything bad or weak away.

Oscar felt like he was shining.

He knew exactly what was going on. Jones and

Northcote were running toward him. The propeller was screaming like a jet plane about to take off. Jones was raising the trumpet and Northcote wanted to grab him, but Oscar didn't care about them. He knew exactly what was going to happen next.

He turned toward them, smiling. He was careful to keep his head low.

Three, two, one . . . , he counted down in his head.

Just as he knew it would, the propeller went into overdrive, spinning so fast it sheered away from the engine.

Jones dived out of the way with catlike grace. Northcote was much less lucky. The propeller caught him in his ample, tweed-jacketed belly and drove him backward.

He smashed into the array of pipes and trumpets that were ranged around Mr. Mortis.

The end was very quick. Just as Northcote himself had said—when a weak ghost is confronted by one of those terrible devices, they vanish pretty quickly. Well, Northcote was weak, and there were at least five Hungry Bottles ravening for his soul.

He disappeared in seconds. He hardly had time to scream.

The remains of the engine exploded, smoke and debris filled the air, glass shattered. Something was burning, but Oscar ignored it. He sprinted over to Sally.

He could barely find her in the smoke—and when he did, he almost missed her, she was that faint.

"Sally!" he shouted.

She didn't reply.

Oscar grabbed one of Mr. Mortis's bell jars full of phantasma and threw it over her. It swirled across her body and disappeared.

"Sally!"

Something magic was happening. Oscar watched her grow more solid. She was filling in, growing thicker and bolder. She was actually there.

There was another huge explosion, but Oscar ignored it. He grabbed her hand.

"Sally!" he shouted. "Can you hear me? Can you see me?"

Sally opened her eyes. She sat up so fast that she almost head-butted Oscar.

"Course I can, you dolt," she said. "Where's Jones?"

"I don't know," Oscar said. There was no sign of the villain, and Oscar couldn't remember what had happened to him. "Should we look for him?"

"No—we need to save Mortis!"

Sally bent over the long form of Mr. Mortis. He was still lying motionless on the floor. She pointed to the bell jar that remained unsmashed.

"You pour that on him," she said. "Lucky you didn't smash it all. Be sharp now. He hasn't got long left."

Oscar didn't dawdle. Mr. Mortis's phantasma jumped

out of the jar as he tipped it over, as if it was eager to get back home. It splashed down on his body like lumpy rain. There was a little flash of golden light as the drops hit, before they were instantly absorbed into his dark suit.

Mr. Mortis gave a long, slow sigh and opened his eyes.

He blinked with surprise. "I'm not dead?" His voice was weak—but there was something familiar about it too. Oscar was sure he'd heard it before.

"No," he said. "You're not."

"And who are you?" Mr. Mortis said. He frowned. "What are you?"

"I'm . . ." Oscar looked for Sally—she'd be better at explaining what had happened, but the detective was gone. She had run over to the shelf of bottles and was searching through them as if her life depended on it.

"What are you doing?" said Oscar, who was still more than a little bewildered by everything.

Sally ignored him and kept on hunting through the shelves.

"Yes!" Suddenly, Sally was screaming in triumph. With great care, she removed two of the bottles from the shelf. "I can save Mum and Dad, Oscar! You did it! We did it!"

"Can someone please explain what is happening?" said Mr. Mortis again. "I thought I was going to Fiji."

CHAPTER
17

It turned out that the God of Death took two sugars in his tea.

"Well, I won't say all of this doesn't come"—Oscar's mum's voice wavered, but she fought on bravely—"as a . . . *teensy* bit of a shock."

She was already on her third cup and had taken the unprecedented step of nibbling on a second cookie. She only did that in moments of the highest stress. The last time Oscar had seen her do it was when their dog had died.

"It'll make sense soon, Mum," he said. "I promise."

It was just about starting to make sense to Oscar. Bright sunshine was streaming into the kitchen. Everything was exactly where it had always been; the striped bread bin with the chipped lid; the dish towel with the picture of the juggling elephant; the very mixed assortment of mugs hanging on hooks beside the sink; the green-and-white-checked tablecloth, still stained where Oscar had spilled a bowl of mushroom soup.

Oscar wanted to lie back and take a bath in the wonderful ordinariness of it all. Everything was in the right place, at last.

His mother reached out, grabbed his hand, and gave it a quick squeeze.

"It sounds like you've been so brave, Osk, and I'm very sorry I called the police on you."

"It doesn't matter, Mum," Oscar said.

"Memory wipes are very powerful, ma'am," added Sally. "It was not your fault at all. Very good work from Northcote."

"Well, that is . . . reassuring," said Mrs. Grimstone, sounding less than totally convinced. Mr. Mortis had granted Mrs. Grimstone the power of phantasmic sight, so she could see him and Sally. She hadn't quite got used to the fact that a ghost detective, who also happened to be a child, was drinking tea at her kitchen table. But that was fair enough. It was a lot to take in. It's not every day that you discover the God of Death is your father-in-law.

"But, my dear, you should be reassured!" Mr. Mortis said, beaming. There was a definite skully quality to him, and although he had a kind face, you were aware of every bone under his skin. "Your son has proved himself in the fiercest of trials. Were it not for him, none of us would be here! Indeed, the world would be in terrible danger. Perhaps ending as we speak, who can say?"

After that dramatic statement, a thinking silence fell on the table. Mr. Mortis took another slurp of tea as they all contemplated the apocalypse that Oscar had narrowly averted.

"I've always known he was special," Mrs. Grimstone said.

The pride in her voice made Oscar blush. "I'm not special, Mum. Don't be silly. It all just happened."

"Poppycock!" Mr. Mortis said, shaking his head.

"Don't listen to him, ma'am," Sally said. "He's done us all proud."

"Oh, Osk!" Mrs. Grimstone was beaming with pride.

"Zounds!" Mr. Mortis leapt to his feet so fast that his chair fell over backward. He was slightly too tall for the room. He was staring at a photograph on the mantelpiece.

"Are you all right, sir?" Sally asked.

Mr. Mortis had turned white. As he was already pretty pale, he looked almost transparent now. He walked carefully across to the mantelpiece.

"Barbara was very special, just like you, Oscar." The photograph showed Oscar's father as a toddler. He was being held by Granny Grimstone. Both of them were grinning out at the camera.

"The only woman I ever loved," Mr. Mortis said. He

sounded close to tears. "When I first saw her in the Christmas market in Vienna . . . I knew for the first time what love was. Imagine! Ten thousand years on Earth—but I'd never felt that fire! That agonizing joy!"

His eyes were very far away.

"Vienna?" Oscar's mum asked. "But Granny said she never left the country!"

"On the contrary, Mrs. Grimstone—she traveled extensively in her youth. . . ." Mr. Mortis shook himself. "But that is an old story for another time. Now is the time to talk of Oscar's future! Which is bright!"

Oscar wasn't sure that was strictly true.

"But first," continued Mr. Mortis, warming to his theme, "we must talk a little about the past. I want to talk about your husband, Mrs. Grimstone, my son, Julian."

"Oh," Oscar's mum said, pulling her mug of tea a little closer. She still hadn't let go of Oscar's hand.

"I loved Julian very much," Mr. Mortis said. "I deeply regret that I could not spend more time with him growing up. My dearest memories are the moments that I snatched to be with him and Barbara. He was a good man."

"I know," Oscar's mum said. Her voice was tight. "Jules was the best."

Oscar gave her hand a squeeze.

"He loved you, Oscar, as much as I loved him. And

when the car crash happened, it was an awful choice he faced. He had no hesitation in choosing to save your life, Oscar, and sacrificing his own."

Tears were running freely down Oscar's mum's cheeks. "Julian did that?" she murmured. "He saved Osk?"

"He did," Mr. Mortis said. "I could not persuade him otherwise."

"I would have done the same," Oscar's mum whispered.

Mr. Mortis turned to Oscar. "Julian used to believe that he was cursed, you know. Just like you. You both had the same problems."

"Things died when he touched them?" Oscar asked.

"Just so." Mr. Mortis nodded. "Both of you carry death in your blood, you see. My gift to you, if you like."

"Some gift," Mrs. Grimstone said.

"Oscar's pretty amazing, ma'am," Sally said. She grinned at Oscar. "You should see him jumping on buses. He's bonkers!"

"Oscar, it is very important," continued Mr. Mortis, "very important indeed, that you learn how to control your powers. And you must learn to extend them too!"

"Well, I can try," said Oscar. There was something a little worrying about the intense way that Mr. Mortis was looking at him.

"Good." Mr. Mortis smiled an awkward, rigid grin.

Again, it wasn't very reassuring. "Because I have learned something during these recent events. Something rather disturbing. Or liberating. It all depends how you look at it."

Mr. Mortis had been pacing restlessly about the kitchen, but now he returned to the mantelpiece and picked up the photograph of Granny Grimstone again.

"The recent unpleasantness wasn't the first time that some angry ghost has tried to kill me, you know. It's happened many times before. Staying a ghost for so long can turn some ghosts a little . . . single-minded, as you can tell from Mr. Northcote. One loses a sense of perspective. The poor man went quite mad. Willing to stop people dying ever again, because he felt underappreciated! There are things that can keep you grounded: spending time with other ghosts, tea, holidays, doing things you enjoy. That sort of thing."

Mr. Mortis seemed to be looking at Sally as he was saying this. He rubbed his chin and continued. "But those other attempts on my life never stood even the slightest chance of succeeding. I am . . . or I should say, I *was* immortal. But Northcote and Jones nearly managed it. In fact, they would have succeeded if you hadn't intervened. I was moments away from the big jump. Moments away from joining Barbara once more. How I long to see her again."

Mr. Mortis closed his eyes and clutched the photograph to his chest.

"As you know, some of my power flowed into my son when I became a father—part of my power was lost. It has had an unintended consequence. It has made me mortal."

Sally gasped. Mrs. Grimstone looked baffled. Oscar had a cold feeling in the pit of his stomach.

"I am aging. My bones ache a little more every morning. I have lived, you know . . . a very long time—and I am getting tired."

"No!" Sally breathed.

"I am going to die," said Mr. Mortis cheerfully. He sounded as if he was announcing that he was popping out to the garden center to pick up a couple of rhododendrons. "It has been a long run—but I am ready. That was the realization I came to in that awful chamber, as they sucked the life out of me. I did not mind, you know. I was quite happy to go."

"You can't!" Sally cried. "You can't do this, sir!"

"I will have to," Mr. Mortis said. "Even I can't cheat death, you see. That's why I need to make some preparations."

He turned to Oscar and smiled at him. It was the least reassuring smile that Oscar had ever seen.

"I need a successor. Would . . . would you, Oscar, consider taking over the Ministry after me?"

The first thought that Oscar had was that this would really put Lady Margaret's nose out of joint. The second, third, fourth, and fifth thoughts were all different colors of utter panic. Purple panic was the worst.

"Urk . . . ," he stammered. He felt like he was going to be sick.

"Of course, I would stick around for a while, to ease the transition," said Mr. Mortis. "You wouldn't be starting cold. But I understand—it's a lot to think about. I'll give you a bit of time to ponder my proposal. Can you let me know by tomorrow morning?"

Oscar Grimstone was pondering all right. He felt like someone who had jumped out of an exploding plane in midair, only to discover that his parachute was made out of lava.

"Would anyone like another cup of tea?" Oscar's mum asked. "I'll put the kettle on."

"If you like, you can work with Sally in the GLE," Mr. Mortis continued. "She's getting a promotion."

"I'm starting the Hieronymus Jones Squad," said Sally. "My parents have agreed to join it. Just as soon as they've properly recovered. We're going to hunt him down like a pack of ravening hyenas. And we need you, Oscar. You're the only ghost—I mean, person—to beat him three times."

The mention of Jones brought Oscar out of his panicked trance. Jones's escape and disappearance lingered like a bad smell in the room.

The villain had tried to kill Oscar three times. He'd brainwashed Oscar's mum and tried to end the world.

He needed to be stopped.

"I'd like that," said Oscar. "In fact, I'd love it."

"Yes, mate!" Sally pounded Oscar on the back. "We'll start tomorrow."

Oscar's mum was pouring boiling water from the kettle.

"That all sounds very nice," she said. "But what about school? Oscar's got his exams coming up."

"His education would come first," Mr. Mortis said smoothly. "Of course schoolwork takes priority!"

School! Oscar had forgotten about school. A few weeks ago, the prospect of going back in September had been about as appealing as an egg-and-crushed-glass burrito, or a maggot bath, or a spritz in the eye with hydrochloric acid.

But now, school didn't seem too bad. All the inevitable jeering and sneering and snide little comments by Oscar's classmates seemed rather pathetic. He didn't think Gary Stevens would be giving him much trouble anymore. Oscar had bigger fish to fry. Hieronymus Jones was about to get turned into an omelet.

Oscar grinned at Sally. Everything was much easier with a real friend, even if she was a ghost.

And if things got bad, Oscar thought, he could just turn

invisible whenever he wanted. That would be a good trick to pull in class.

"I've still got a few more weeks of summer holiday," he said. "Forget tomorrow. Let's get hunting right away!"

"That's the ticket!" Sally said.

Oscar's mum was pouring steaming tea into his mug. Oscar took a big sip and felt the familiar warmth seep through his body.

It tasted like victory.

ABOUT THE AUTHOR

Andrew Prentice is the author of two critically acclaimed YA historical novels, *Black Arts* and *Devil's Blood*. *Black Arts* was shortlisted for the Branford Boase Award and longlisted for the Carnegie Medal. He has also written for comics and animation. *Ghost and Bone* is his first middle-grade novel.